THE OLD MAN'S PLACE

Books by John Sanford

Make My Bed in Hell
The People from Heaven
A Man Without Shoes
The Land that Touches Mine
Every Island Fled Away
The $300 Man
A More Goodly Country
Adirondack Stories
View from this Wilderness
To Feed Their Hopes
The Winters of that Country
William Carlos Williams/John Sanford: A Correspondence
The Color of the Air
The Waters of Darkness
A Very Good Land to Fall Wit
A Walk in the Fire
The Season, It Was Winter
Maggie: A Love Story,
The View from Mt. Morris
We Have a Little Sister
Intruders in Paradise
A Palace of Silver
Speaking in an Empty Room: The Selected Letters of John Sanford

As Julian L. Shapiro

The Water Wheel

THE OLD MAN'S PLACE

JOHN SANFORD

ISBN-13: 978-1-7358517-3-0

Published by
Brash Books
PO Box 8212
Calabasas, CA 91372
www.brash-books.com

This book is for "THE GOVERNOR"

INTRODUCTION TO THE NEW EDITION BY JACK MEARNS

*T*he Old Man's Place is, first and foremost, a rip-roaring tale of moral bankruptcy, violence and mayhem. From the outset, author John Sanford creates an ominous tension, as a depraved trio of World War One veterans descends upon the Adirondack Mountains farm on which one of them grew up. Havoc reigns, until the arrival of a naive mail-order bride speeds the novel to its bloody climax. From that synopsis, it should be clear that any devotee of hard-boiled crime fiction will delight in this fast-paced narrative of vice about the return of an unrepentant prodigal son and his vicious cohorts. Beneath the thrilling surface, though, *The Old Man's Place* can be read as a crucial turning-point in the work of its author—away from the preoccupations of his youth— a book that would make possible a new life he could never have imagined.

John Sanford was born Julian Shapiro in 1904 in Harlem, NY, then a fashionable Jewish enclave. His mother had been born in Manhattan's Lower East Side. His father had immigrated from Russia as a youth—first helping out in the family butcher shop and then apprenticing with an uncle to become a lawyer. By the time of Julian's birth, the father had a successful law practice working with the burgeoning Jewish building trade in the city. However, two events shook the family's world. First, the financial panic of 1907 wiped out the father's legal work, leaving the family destitute. And then, when Julian was ten years old, his mother died following a lengthy illness.

In the years after his mother's death, Julian Shapiro was recalcitrant and adrift. He felt alienated from his father and did poorly in school. As a teen, he ran away from home, bumming his way to Florida, where he spent a night in jail for vagrancy. Eventually, he decided to turn his aimless and headstrong life around by following his father's example. He enrolled in Fordham Law School, whose classes were held on the 28th floor of the Woolworth skyscraper in downtown Manhattan.

It was during his law studies that a chance encounter on a New Jersey golf course altered the path of his life. While playing by himself, Shapiro happened upon another solitary golfer, whom he recognized from his Harlem youth, Nathan Weinstein. However, the man was now calling himself Nathanael West. Shapiro proudly told West that he was becoming a lawyer, but West's reply stunned him: "I'm writing a book." At that moment, legal studies lost their luster, and the idea of writing a book tantalized Shapiro.

Back in New York, West and Shapiro became frequent companions, with West lecturing his new acolyte about art and literature during long walks around the city. Shapiro read proof with West several times on his first novel, *The Dream Life of Balso Snell*. And in the summer of 1931, the pair departed New York City to write in a rented hunting cabin on Viele Pond in the Adirondack hamlet of Warrensburg. West worked on his second novel, *Miss Lonelyhearts*, while Shapiro revised his first, *The Water Wheel*. Those four months were transformative for Shapiro, as he devoted himself full-time to writing and soaked up the region's local color. Shapiro would go on to set his next three novels in Warrensburg, a trilogy in which he bored deeply into the troubled American psyche that lay beneath a pastoral surface.

Upon returning from the country, Shapiro began to work on a new novel. The plot was based on a story the owner of the Viele Pond lodge, Harry Reoux, had told Shapiro about a group of poachers who terrorized the area. Originally titled *The Trampled Vineyard*, it eventually became *The Old Man's Place*, and the poachers became ex-soldiers. Over two months in the fall of 1931, Sanford completed a first draft, writing on the roof of Manhattan's Sutton Hotel, which West managed.

The Old Man's Place marked a stark shift in Shapiro's prose. *The Water Wheel* is a novel modernist in its aims, with lofty artistic intentions. Heavily influenced by James Joyce's stream of consciousness work, the autobiographical *Water Wheel* takes place largely in the head of its protagonist, John Sanford, a young New York lawyer with ambitions to give up the legal trade and become a writer. Shapiro eschewed quote marks and apostrophes and filled the novel with self-conscious flourishes and wordplay. Published in 1933 by Dragon Press in an edition of a few hundred copies, it had no chance of commercial success. In fact, after the publisher went belly up, the book's bindery came after Shapiro to cover printing expenses Dragon had defaulted on.

After being admitted to the bar, Shapiro joined his father's law office. However, the Depression once again decimated the father's practice, and there was little legal work to be done. By 1935, Shapiro's father's repeated losses had weakened him; early that year, he suffered a series of heart attacks, leaving him hospitalized. Shapiro's aunt implored her nephew to give up his unremunerative avocation and devote himself to resuscitating the father's moribund practice to bring some money home. However, Shapiro stubbornly rejected her pleas and continued writing.

Despite his refusal to bow to his family's economic pressures, book sales were clearly on Shapiro's mind, for the style of *The Old Man's Place* is the polar opposite of *The Water Wheel's*. While the first novel is interior to Sanford's mind—plumbing his diffidence and passivity—*The Old Man's Place* is lurid with overt and violent criminal action. On the whole, the novel's prose is spare, direct and unembellished, allowing the plot to propel the novel with ferocious intensity.

Still, there are a few unobtrusive holdovers from Shapiro's earlier style, such as running together several words to make a single adjective—e.g., "chlorinatedwaterblue eyes"—and the occasional artful expression, like "clouds slitting their bellies on the blades" of mountain ridges. Sanford's summer at Viele Pond bore fruit in lovely evocations of Nature and the landscape. Finally, although far from autobiographical, it is not hard to see a penitent son's regret over his wayward and defiant youth as seeding Trubee Pell's shiftlessness and dishonoring of his father.

The completed novel was placed with Albert and Charles Boni by Shapiro's cousin Mel Friedman, who also is credited with its typography. It was the first book the house had published in three years. Boni offered Shapiro a $100 advance and a promise of $100 more upon receiving a revision of the manuscript. At age 30, that was the first money Shapiro had earned from writing. Based on West's suggestion, Shapiro decided to adopt a pseudonym to avoid the reading public's potential bias against buying a book by a Jewish author. He chose John Sanford, the name of his *Water Wheel* alter-ego. Not only did Shapiro choose a pen name: he invented an entire authorial character he sought to root deeply in the American grain. The rear panel of the dust jacket completes his transformation by printing a swaggering letter from "Jack Sanford" that mixes fact and fiction to describe Jack London-esque adventures and proclaims his aspiration to write a "book as American as [Mathew] Brady's pictures."

The Old Man's Place was released in October 1935. In his autobiography, John Sanford wrote of admiring his cousin's typography but otherwise feeling disappointed with the novel physically. It was smaller than the typical book of the time, and Sanford disliked the binding, which he found crude. In particular, he thought the dust jacket art looked cheap, with its starkly etched trio of toughs—one clutching a booze bottle in his fist—looming over a sun-dappled farm in the background. To my mind, though, the illustration evokes a sense of menace and accurately captures the characters—the animalistic predation of Martin Flood, the obsequiousness of James Pilgrim, and the aloof indifference of Trubee Pell.

Reviews of *The Old Man's Place* were mixed. Some reviewers rejected the novel with repugnance for the depravity of the characters and the violence of the plot (e.g., one review titled "A Horrid, Horrid Book about Horrible Men"). However, The Cleveland *Plain Dealer* found a glimmer of redemption in the prose:

> As for fiction, the most striking example I have run across is *The Old Man's Place*, by John Sanford. In an era of brutal fiction, *The Old Man's Place* will take a prize for brutality. If there be tenderness among the sons of men, if there be mercy, if there be any pity or forbearance, or even a shuddering away from the more obscenely ruthless acts of gratuitous savagery, such effeminate weakness has no place between the covers of this sadistic novel. But...this John Sanford writes well. He has a talent for it: he is vivid, realistic, skillful, dramatic.

Reviewers noted similarities in theme to the work of William Faulkner, Ernest Hemingway, James M. Cain and Erskine Caldwell, one stating that Sanford could "hold his own with any of his contemporaries of high rank."

Others wrote: "A mediocre writer would certainly make a melodramatic mess of this material, but Sanford has achieved the heights of drama" and "Sanford is a supreme master at squeezing the last drop of terror and excitement out of a sordid, savage situation. Until the bitter end, the story sweeps along with an ugly force that will send sensitive souls in search of the smelling salts." A New York *Times* review began: "Here is a first-rate piece of swift-moving and dramatic story-telling in restrained and effective modern American prose," but it faulted the book as superficial, lacking meaning. Another review compared Sanford's "easy colloquial American idiom" to William Carlos Williams's short stories, calling *The Old Man's Place* "a work of very genuine skill and feeling."

The highly influential New York *Times* reviewer John Chamberlain opined that Sanford "is to the novel what the school of Thomas Benton or Grant Wood is to painting—a 'nativist' who takes a purely aesthetic delight in the salt and savor, even the occasional flaring of brutality, of the American character." Chamberlain also explicitly tied the veterans' viciousness to their experiences overseas in the war, their "having seen the practice of international gangsterism at close range." In later years, Sanford's primary regret about the book was that he had not made *The Old Man's Place* an anti-war novel by more explicitly connecting the characters' wickedness to their dehumanizing participation in war.

Despite Sanford's high hopes and some positive press, *The Old Man's Place* sold just 1,055 copies. Undaunted, Sanford began his third novel. At that time, he was living with his father, who was now convalescing at home, and filching fifteen cents a day from the father's change pocket to cover expenses—a dime for a half-pack of cigarettes and a nickel for a towel at the YMCA following a game of handball. One morning, Sanford's handball match was interrupted by an urgent message to call home. Fearing the worst about his father's health, Sanford was relieved when his father answered the phone, delivering the news that, on the basis of *The Old Man's Place*, Paramount Pictures offered Sanford a screenwriting contract: $350 a week for six months, with the option to renew, plus a train ticket to Los Angeles.

Sanford's transit from Depression-era New York to Hollywood could not have felt any less magical than Dorothy's finding herself no longer in Kansas. The 32-year-old man, who had been financially dependent on his father, was now earning a handsome salary—enough to buy a car and new clothes, send money back to New York, and sock away savings for the future. At Paramount, the novice was teamed first with Joseph Moncure March, the original editor of *The New Yorker*, and later with Lynn Riggs, the American Indian playwright. Neither partnership resulted in a script that made it to the screen. Outside of work, though, Sanford briefly dated starlet Jean Muir and regularly rounded out guest lists for dinner at Joan Crawford's house. Most importantly, Sanford met in a Paramount hallway an up-and-coming screenwriter, Marguerite Roberts, whom he would marry in 1939.

After six months, Paramount granted Sanford another half-year's employment but soon regretted their offer, as no usable script emerged. Except for co-writing the Clark Gable/Lana Turner Western *Honky Tonk* with Roberts in 1941, Sanford never again worked in the movies. Roberts, though, became one of Hollywood's highest paid screenwriters and supported Sanford for the rest of his life, allowing him to devote himself completely to writing books.

The copyright for *The Old Man's Place* was taken out in Boni's name. After World War Two, Sanford set about obtaining from publishers the copyrights to his early books. However, Boni refused to hand over the rights; because there were copies available for sale, the book was technically still in print. In fact, earlier, Boni had even asserted ownership of the fiction that was "John Sanford," seeking unsuccessfully to prevent the author from publishing more books using that name. In 1948, Sanford arranged with Pickwick Books in Hollywood to purchase all 350 remaining copies of *The Old Man's Place*; he then demanded that Boni either run a second printing or surrender the copyright. Under protest, the publisher relinquished the rights to the book to Sanford.

In the 1950's, *The Old Man's Place* was reprinted twice as a pulp paperback—in 1953 by Permabooks under the original title, and in 1957 by Signet as *The Hard Guys*. Signet reported selling nearly 156,000 copies. In 1972, an uninspiring film adaptation was produced, variously called *My Old Man's Place* and *Glory Boy*. The movie starred William Devane and Michael Moriarty, and it altered the time and place to Vietnam-era California. In 1982, Black Sparrow sold off Sanford's long-stored copies of the original Boni edition.

After *The Old Man's Place*, Sanford would go on to write 22 more books, including his superb five-volume autobiography, *Scenes from the Life of an American Jew*. None of those books would have been possible had it not been for *The Old Man's Place*—the key that unlocked Sanford's future. In *The Old Man's Place* we can see the nascent themes that would flourish in the next two installments of his Warrensburg trilogy, *Seventy Times Seven* and *The People from Heaven*, and preoccupy him for the rest of his career. *The Old Man's Place* also represents a clear pivot toward Sanford's mature writing style.

But, beyond its being a steppingstone on the way to greater things, *The Old Man's Place* is worthy in its own right—a gripping, well-told yarn that takes the reader on a wild ride. It is high time for this compelling novel to be in the hands of the public again.

Jack Mearns is a professor of psychology at California State University, Fullerton. He is the author of John Sanford: An Annotated Bibliography (Oak Knoll Press, 2008).

Books by John Sanford

Novels and Stories

1933: *The Water Wheel*, Dragon (reissued 2020 by Tough Poets)

1935: *The Old Man's Place*, Albert & Charles Boni (reissued 1953 by Permabooks; 1957 as *The Hard Guys* by Signet; 2021 by Brash)

1939: *Seventy Times Seven*, Knopf (reissued 1954 & 1957 as *Make My Bed in Hell* by Avon; 2021 by Brash)

1943: *The People from Heaven*, Harcourt, Brace (reissued 1995 by University of Illinois)

1951: *A Man Without Shoes*, Plantin (reissued 1982 by Black Sparrow; 2013 by Bloomsbury Reader [e-book])

1953: *The Land that Touches Mine*, Doubleday & Jonathan Cape

1964: *Every Island Fled Away*, Norton

1967: *The $300 Man*, Prentice-Hall

1976: *Adirondack Stories*, Capra

Creative Interpretations of History

1975: *A More Goodly Country*, Horizon

1977: *View from this Wilderness*, Capra

1980: *To Feed Their Hopes*, University of Illinois (reissued 1995 as *A Book of American Women* by University of Illinois)

1984: *The Winters of that Country*, Black Sparrow

1997: *Intruders in Paradise*, University of Illinois

Autobiography, Memoir and Letters

1984: *William Carlos Williams/John Sanford: A Correspondence*, Oyster

1985: *The Color of the Air*, Black Sparrow

1986: *The Waters of Darkness*, Black Sparrow

1987: *A Very Good Land to Fall With*, Black Sparrow

1989: *A Walk in the Fire*, Black Sparrow

1991: *The Season, It Was Winter*, Black Sparrow

1993: *Maggie: A Love Story*, Barricade (reissued 2013 by Bloomsbury Reader [e-book])

1994: *The View from Mt. Morris*, Barricade

1995: *We Have a Little Sister*, Capra

2003: *A Palace of Silver*, Capra (reissued 2013 by Bloomsbury Reader [e-book])

2021: *Speaking in an Empty Room: The Selected Letters of John Sanford*, Tough Poets

PUBLISHER'S NOTE

It is a pleasure to bring back into print a crime-writing masterpiece—*The Old Man's Place* by John Sanford. This hardboiled classic, originally published in 1935, showcases Sanford as a supreme stylist, who crafted sentences not only in terms of what the words mean but also for how they sound to the ear and look to the eye on the page. We see this craft, in particular, in Sanford's combining words in unusual ways, such as "brightgreen" or "kitchenknife." While these artistic elements may initially surprise readers, they will enhance the overall reading experience. John Sanford has been described as America's "most outstanding neglected novelist." With this Brash Books edition, we aim to end this neglect!

CHAPTER ONE

L ate at night, in a waterfront saloon a few doors off West Street, three men sat around the wet marble slab of a small table near a nickelodeon opposite the bar. The only customers in the place, they showed no sign of leaving even though for some time the bartender had been trying to make it plain to them that he wanted to close up and go home. One of the men looked across the room at him, holding up three fingers. The bartender stared for several seconds before taking a bottle over to the table and refilling the glasses.

The three men were James Pilgrim, Martin Flood and Trubee Pell.

James Pilgrim, now thirty years old, was born in 1890 in the hall bedroom of a boardinghouse near Chatham Square. His father, an oiler on the South American freighter "Roanoke," had spent a few nights with a fat thrush that he'd met in a Mott Street beer hall. A week later, bound for Montevideo with a cargo of farm machinery, the "Roanoke" had plodded through the Narrows and out past Sandy Hook, but not before the woman had made the oiler promise to marry her when his ship came back to port. Many weeks afterward she realized that it was a mistake to have taken the word for the deed; discovering that the oiler had left something behind, she sat down and cursed him out for a solid hour. She was wasting her time, however, for the oiler was at the bottom of the South Atlantic Ocean with a cargo of farm machinery lying on his chest.

At the age of eleven, James got tired of spending all his time around the Home in which his mother had been boarding him since she entered Mrs. Janeway's, a thirdclass establishment located close to the Astor House and catering to a trade composed mainly of brokendown lawyers in greasy Prince Alberts and wardheelers in chamberpot derbies. The Home was in Jersey City at the rim of the Hackensack Meadows, and from his window James had often watched the long strings of freightcars moving in the deep lanes cut through the rushes and marsh grass. He'd wondered what was in the cars, in the thousands of them that he'd seen crawling toward him and then away from him day after day. He'd wondered most where they were going. He didn't care where they'd come from; he didn't even think about that. All he wanted to find out was what happened to the cars after they'd passed him and gone out of sight in the oilgreen mist that always hung over the marshes, and one night, after all the other boys were asleep, he made a bundle of the few clothes he owned, let himself out of the Home through the cellardoor, and headed across the Meadows toward a distant strip of ballast.

In a few moments he was lost among the sixfoot reeds, and then for hours he waded ankledeep in the muck, searching for the right of way he believed he'd marked the afternoon before. Wandering about in the darkness, he fell into a drainage canal and lost his bundle during the struggle to get through the slow-flowing chinhigh brook of petroleum and waste water, and after that he moved in circles for the rest of the night until the lightening sky over the Palisades showed him that he was on an island in the swamp. Beyond the brook, just above the swaying cylinders of cat tail, he saw the faint gleam of the rails, and then once more he went into the thick black syrup of the canal.

A long walk down the ties brought him to a siding on which a train of boxcars stretched away into the earlymorning mist as far as he could see. He climbed into the empty refrigerator of a fruit express and almost instantly fell asleep on the damp slats that covered the floor. A few hours later, before the train got under way, a railroad detective discovered the sleeping figure in the ice-box; instead of taking the boy into custody, he closed the hatch overhead and locked it from the outside. The boy was imprisoned for three days, but managed to last by prying up some of the slats and drinking the rank icewater that'd collected above a plugged drain. A brakeman in the Louisville yards heard him beating against the tin walls of the compartment, pulled him out by the hair, and booted him off the train.

At the racetrack at Churchill Downs, the boy got a job with the Forshay Farms, an outfit owned by a meatpacker from Chicago, and for the next two years he worked in the stables sweeping the droppings out of the stalls, washing down the boards and padding, and tossing hay out of the lofts to make fresh bedding for the Forshay thoroughbreds. The work hardened him, but it added very little to his height, and by the time he'd reached the age of fourteen he was as tall as he'd ever be in his life.

Because of his size, he liked to imagine himself a member of the little band of jockeys who drove up to the Forshay tackroom every morning in their private carriages, but all of his attempts to become friendly with the riders ended in his being treated like a servant, and once, making the blunder of addressing one of them in front of the Seelbach Hotel in Louisville, he was at first ignored, and then he was caned into the gutter when he persisted.

He took away from that scene no ill feeling against the jockey for having disgraced him in public. He didn't know that he'd been disgraced; he understood the flogging to be the natural result of his having dared to speak to a gentleman, and he admitted to himself that if their positions had been reversed he'd have taken his stick and broken it over the jockey's head for the insult. A stable boy was low company for anyone to be seen with, but some day he'd be a jockey, too; some day he'd be a gentleman and cane an upstart in front of a fashionable hotel with dozens of fashionable men and women standing around and watching him prove to them that he was one of their kind.

He overlooked no chance to nag the trainers to put him up on a horse, on any horse, even one of the unsound platers they campaigned for Forshay at county fairs in the grain belt of the middle west, and after a while, more to stop his constant begging than to see whether he had riding ability, they put him in charge of a fiveyearold that was still a maiden after racing almost all its life against the cheapest competition on the track.

The boy treated the animal as if it were the finest and fastest thoroughbred ever developed in America. He starved himself in order to have enough money to buy the choicest feed for it, and when he brought it out for exercise at dawn it was as carefully groomed as if it were running in a Derby. Nobody around his stable paid much attention to him, but one day the meatpacker came down from Chicago to inspect his horses and happened to see the boy riding his plater over to the training track. Following him, the meatpacker was treated to an exhibition of horsemanship that convinced him that the boy would eventually make a firstclass jockey.

When the other riders found out that Forshay had taken up with the stable boy, they went out of their way to be sociable, even the one who'd thrashed him in front of the Seelbach the year before. They taught him all they knew, and to this he added a good deal more of his own, and when, one afternoon at Pimlico, he rode his fortieth winner and lost his apprenticeship, he felt that at last he'd realized the ambition of his life, to be a jockey and a gentleman. That evening he was called "Mister" for the first time, and he fell so in love with the title that he wouldn't have changed places with a king.

He was then a little over seventeen, and signing a contract with Forshay, he rode for him on every decent track in the country from Gravesend all the way to Oakland. By the time he'd been twice around the circuit, there were very few who failed to address him in the proper manner. He insisted on it, even to the point where he once turned his back on Forshay for having so far forgotten himself as to omit the "Mister"; he prized the designation so highly that it was impossible for him to hear enough of it, and it wasn't very long before a smart gambler discovered how simple it was to "Mister" the boy into overlooking the fact that he was employed by Forshay.

Pilgrim wasn't suspected until one summer afternoon at Lexington in 1908, when he rode a favorite for Forshay and did everything but toss himself out of the saddle. He cost the meat-packer a fortune with this performance, but it was one of the trainers who hailed him just as he was stepping off the scales and took the long chance of ramming his hand into the jockey's boot; it came out with a ticket on the winning horse. Then, right beneath the railing of the Judges' stand, the trainer knocked the boy down, pulled off the boot, and poured out the rest of the bribe. Before lodging a complaint with the Judges, the trainer leaned over and smashed the jockey across the mouth with the heel of the boot. The trainer was suspended for this, but he counted the punishment as well worthwhile when the Jockey Club announced that it'd ruled Mister Pilgrim off the turf for life.

From that time on, the boy went downhill. When he sought out the gambler who'd been paying him to lose, he found that the man couldn't remember his name, much less his title, and for years afterward he listened for it in vain from everyone he encountered, from beggars in the street, from blind men, from people who stopped him to ask for directions, from the women along Ninth Avenue who wouldn't speak to him at all unless he approached them with a twodollar bill in his hand.

He made a living by doing odd jobs and running errands for a gang of toughs who worked the small shopkeepers in the Chelsea district with an extortion trick that consisted of selling promises not to throw bricks through the storefronts. Never a member of the gang, he hung around with them only long enough to learn their methods and a few of their ideas. When he did, he took an unimportant confidence game on tour with him, making Easton, Pennsylvania, as the first stop of his trip. It was also the last, for the night he arrived he had the bad luck to try to rook the one man in the lobby of the Huntingdon who was there on similar business; the man asked Pilgrim to be good enough to take a walk with him, and when they reached the first corner four knuckles squashed the exjockey's lips into a pulp against his teeth.

Leaving Easton, he headed south and knocked about the Maryland racetracks, earning his bread and butter by selling tips to bettors. When the season ended, he made his way back to New York, and no sooner had he turned up in his old neighborhood than he was arrested on an indictment charging him with extortion. He knew very well that his tough cronies had managed to throw the blame for their crimes on him, and he also knew that he'd gain nothing and possibly lose his life if he tried to pay them back in their own coin. By pleading guilty on all counts, and later by behaving himself while at Elmira, he was out of prison in a little less than two years.

In a few months he was back again for the felony of carrying a gun after having been convicted of a crime, and this time he spent three years in jail. Between 1914 and 1917, drunkenness and petty larceny kept him so much on the move between Blackwell's Island and Manhattan that one of the wardens called him "The Commuter" and assigned him to cell number 515.

Absolutely penniless after his last release from the Island, he borrowed a gun and took the desperate chance of holding up a crap game in the basement of a political club on Bleecker Street, a game that he knew was being run by some of his old friends from Chelsea. Recognizing his frightened voice through the rag he wore tied around his face, they gave him an hour's headstart with a hatful of bills before following him to his basement room on Bethune Street and turning him into such a hamburger with their hands and heels that it was hard to tell where his head ended and his body began. After that, dragging him around to a recruiting station at the corner of Christopher and Greenwich, they stood by while he signed away three more years of his life.

They didn't call him "Mister" in the army. When they found out that he was an exjockey, they called him "Turd" and sent him back to where he'd started—in the stables piling manure. On account of his size, he did more fighting with a broom than a rifle, and he was still busy sweeping when the war ended.

James "Turd" Pilgrim was a homely little man standing about five feet three. Because of his habit of muzzling every dray-horse he passed in the street, he almost always carried about with him the stink of stables, sweaty harness, and stale urine. His long thin face was littered with a confetti of yellow pimples that made it look like a coatcollar during a carnival. His eyes seemed to be solid brown, horsebrown, and his wobbly lips, even in his sleep, were always damp with the beer of his saliva. The teeth he still had in his skull were as green as slime, and they turned black where they entered his gums; those in front were as granular as melting sugar, and tapered to points as if they'd been whittled down like pencils. He'd been told by an army dentist that it'd be a good idea for him to shop around for a comfortable set of plates unless he felt like eating oatmeal during all the time he was in France, but the cavalry mounts had kept him working over-time in the stables and he'd had no chance to equip himself with store teeth before his outfit sailed. He'd left several of his decayed splinters of bone lying around Europe, with the result that when he came back his upper lip was beginning to overlap his lower one. He was a homely little man.

The three men were James Pilgrim, Martin Flood, and Trubee Pell.

Martin Flood hailed from a waterhole in western Nebraska about three hundred miles from Omaha. He was four years older than Pilgrim and at least four times as strong; he'd always been strong, even when he was a boy, even when he was only up to long division and his father had taken him out of school because another hand was needed around the farm. For more than twenty years after that Flood pitched hay and sawed wood, and in that time, pound by pound, he lifted thousands of tons of dead weight to help his father transform the prairie into a garden. They never succeeded, but the hard work gave Flood a life so good that he'd have boiled off the creamy surface of it every night in the year if he'd gotten the chance, but because the farm was so far from its neighbors he had to let the heat of the sun dry him up for six straight days before each Saturday afternoon turned him loose to run wild through the thick layer of dust that buried the plains. Saturday night after Saturday night, for the last fifteen years he spent on the farm, he stayed with every woman he could lay his hands on within ten miles of his home—over and over again, Saturday night after Saturday night. That was all he did—pitch hay, saw wood, plow the fields, and stay with women for long nights of almost unbroken struggle to lose something that refused to be lost—each regularly, each in its turn, without a break for fifteen years. Martin Flood was a farmer.

He'd never been sick a day in his life. The hard work, the soggy farm food, the still soggier Scandinavian whores who liked the way he could smell them out across miles and miles of prairie grass and sand—nothing had ever given him as much as a headache. He liked his life well enough to stay behind when the patriots enlisted at the beginning of the war; he waited for the draft, and his number was drawn during the summer of 1917. He was sorry when the time came for him to leave the farm, but later on, over in France, he found out that the French girls, even the flabby old ones with bright red frizzed hair, even the fat ones who rouged their nipples until they glared like headlights, knew a trick or two that ruined his memories of the Swedish cows that'd lain under him like the earth, like soft damp quilts of spongy moss. He was sorry when he had to come back to America; nearly every night had been Saturday night, and he still hadn't been sick a day in his life.

Martin Flood was built like an inverted steeple. His shoulders spread at right angles from a throat as thick as a hydrant, and his arms took a long fall from the isosceles pyramid of his body, ending in hands the size of boxing gloves. He was six feet tall and weighed a hundred and ninetyfive pounds. It'd taken him a long time to find out what a soft life it was for a strong man, and now that he knew it he wasn't the sucker to go back to Nebraska and try to plow a living out of the desert. That kind of stuff was for rubes; as far as he was concerned, he was going to take his ease from that time on, and there'd be plenty of handy people around to take hold of the dirty end of the stick while he watched them and handed out orders. Martin Flood was no longer a farmer.

The three men were James Pilgrim, Martin Flood, and Trubee Pell.

Trubee Pell, five years younger than Pilgrim, was the only son of Walter Pell, a farmer whose property was on the Viele Pond road, eight miles out of Warrensburg, New York. The farm had been in the family since 1777, when Trubee's greatgrandfather, a grenadier with Fraser's division, had escaped from Saratoga after Burgoyne's surrender and beaten his way back north with a pack of friendly Algonquins. He'd swapped them his uniform for the tract of land, built a shack for himself in a little clearing along Stewart Brook, found a wife at Fort William Henry the following spring, and then chunk by chunk he and his descendants had carved fields out of a wilderness of beech and maple.

Trubee's mother had died of a hemorrhage an hour after he was born, and his father was left with the job of bringing up the child and running the farm. For the first couple of months, the wife of a neighbor named Bennett did what she could to help Pell get straightened out, but after that, although the Bennetts advised him to board the child some place until it was old enough to take care of itself, he insisted on looking after his own no matter what it was going to cost him to do it.

If he'd had to work hard before his wife's death, then he nearly broke his back on the farm afterward. For years there wasn't a night that he had more than five hours' sleep, and not a single day off did he take until Trubee finished his first year at grade school. Then he invited the Bennetts and the Slocums over to the house, and they all had a blowout, a mild and tired one, but a blowout just the same.

Trubee and his father saw very few people during the course of a year, but those who came across the boy and had a chance to get friendly with him usually told the old man that he'd done a pretty good job of raising his son, that he could hardly have done better even if he'd had his wife to help him; they said that if Trubee listened to reason and did the right thing, he might amount to something some day—might get to be a figure in the county, they said, might even be sent down to Albany.

Nothing could have given old man Pell more satisfaction than talk like that. For some reason that he'd never been able to put into words, he'd always had a special interest in Trubee over and above the one that a father usually had in his son. This interest might have been due to a feeling of guilt about the death of his wife, it might have been due to some quality that he either saw in the boy or wanted him to have, and again it might have been only another form of his fear that the farm would slip away from the family and fall into strange hands; but whatever it was, only on the last point could the old man find anything to say.

At the bottom of all the lectures that he ever gave Trubee was the idea that no man had any real right to hold his head up unless he had a piece of land that he could call his own. It didn't make any difference how small or poor the land was, he used to tell Trubee, and it didn't make any difference what the man had to go through to hold on to it; as long as he and his family didn't have to pay rent or mortgage money to some landshark for leave to have a roof over their heads, they were as good as anybody on the face of the earth, and better than most because they didn't live off other people's sweat; they took their living right out of the ground, their own ground, and they took out just what they put in, and no more.

Trubee grew up in the woods surrounding the farm. Not a day went by but he was off somewhere ploughing through the brush, watching birds and small game with an old telescope that his father had given him for a birthday present, hunting the country and fishing every stream deep enough to float a plug, tramping over all the mountains and through all the forests within twenty miles of Viele Pond. At the age of fifteen, he knew more about the woods than he did about his own face. The things he knew were of the private kind that only long familiarity with the neighborhood could have taught him: although he'd never shot a deer, he knew the only saltlick in the district where he could see one almost any time he wanted to, and more than once he'd had the excitement of sitting in plain view of the lick while a deer was feeding; he knew the pools in Stewart Brook where the largest trout were to be found; he had his own spring that he'd stocked with minnows for bass fishing, and he knew an unbeatable bass bunk, a very small pond only three miles away from the farm across the mountains, but so hard to get to that he went there only when he had the whole day to spare; and, what was rarest of all, he knew a nest that for five years running had been used by the same pair of duckhawks, a brace of birds that'd gotten to know him so well that he could climb up the cliff to the very ledge they were perched on before they took wing.

As Trubee grew older, particularly during the two years that he went to high school, his father became more and more careful with him. In the long run, the boy always took Pell's orders, but at school he'd begun to do some thinking for himself, and he now put up an argument whenever what his father told him ran counter to his own ideas. As far as Trubee was concerned, none of the arguments amounted to very much, and the old man's taking them so seriously put him out a good deal more than he felt like admitting; there was no reason, he thought, for his father to carry on each and every time he wanted to make a little trip to Warrensburg, and there was no reason for the doses of advice he used to get before setting out and the third degrees he was put through after coming home.

When Trubee was out of sight, Pell worried himself to a frazzle. He was always afraid that some woman who was no good would take a fancy to the boy, or that Trubee would start drinking and do something that he'd regret for the rest of his life; he was always afraid that Trubee would run up against one of the many temptations that, as he often said, lay in wait for young men and lured them on to ruin. He spoke of these temptations as if they had length, breadth, and thickness, as if, although they went about dressed in clothes, they were just too foxy for any young boy to reckon with. Where all these temptations were to be found among the four hundred and fifty people who lived in Warrensburg, Pell didn't stop to figure out. All he knew was that whenever he let Trubee go down to the village after dark, he sat around chewing his nails off until the boy came home.

There was another thing that Pell overlooked, and that was that Trubee was just about as levelheaded as they came. He never drank, and no amount of kidding by his friends could make him touch anything stronger than root beer. He had his first woman when he was sixteen, but his luck was pretty good and nothing very much happened either to turn him sour or to make him treat women any better than they deserved. Several of the girls in Warrensburg tried to shine up to him because they couldn't seem to get him excited over them; the reason he didn't let them bother him was that he'd found a steady, the daughter of a man who ran a service station on the Chestertown road, and he stuck to her for a number of years without making the affair so noticeable that it was talked about in the village. In fact, he took so little part in conversations about women that his friends used to josh him for being on the good side and ask him the name of the body he was saving it all up for. Once in a while they came out with a remark about his keeping pretty close to his father's suspenders, but he took it all in good fun and got as big a laugh out of their digs as anybody else who'd heard them.

For all his crossexamining, the old man never caught on to these things about Trubee, and no matter what he'd been told he always fancied the worst—that with each visit to town the boy was getting closer to ruination—and finally one night when Trubee came home late after a heavy downpour that'd kept him away a couple of hours longer than he usually stayed, Pell let out his first hint that he wouldn't mind Trubee's seeing a little more of Esther Pirie, a girl whose father had a good farm in the valley near Thurman Station.

Toward the end of 1916, when it began to look as if the United States were going to get mixed up in the war sooner or later, the old man did some more worrying about Trubee. He said nothing to the boy about it, but figuring that the time was ripe for him to settle down, he got together with Esther's father and talked business. The upshot of the meeting was the making of a deal by the two farmers. Immediately afterward, Pell began to drop in a good word for Esther here and there, and several times in his talks with Trubee he found openings for stating what a high opinion he had of her family. Trubee got the old man's drift after a while, and more to put an end to the hinting than to start in keeping company, he called on Esther a few times a month during the winter of that year.

The day the United States declared war Trubee went to his father and asked him for permission to enlist. From the way the idea was treated, Trubee gathered that his father thought he was joking. He went to Warrensburg that evening to get the papers and the latest news, talked to some friends who were going to join up in a day or two, and then returned to the farm. Again he asked for his father's permission, and this time Pell saw that Trubee was in earnest. He put up a terrible holler and carried on as if the boy had asked him to consent to his committing suicide. He got so bad, finally, that Trubee had to walk out of the room. The boy didn't stop trying, though, and day after day he thought up new arguments to put to the old man, hoping to get him to change his mind. After a week of quarreling, Pell came straight out with the remark that the only way Trubee could enlist was over his father's dead body. Realizing then that he'd never get his father's consent, and not being the kind to go without it, Trubee was ready for anything the old man suggested. The suggestion was that Trubee get married to Esther Pirie.

The marriage took place on the morning of May 1st, 1917. Trubee and his wife were to start off on a short wedding trip that afternoon, and when the ceremony was over he went down to Warrensburg to buy a few things that he needed for the journey. Passing the Post Office, he saw a crowd of his friends standing out in front; they were looking at the New York papers and reading the latest bulletins that'd been chalked on the slate that hung between the two front windows of the building. Trubee greeted the fellows as he went by. Getting no answer, he turned back to find out what was the matter. One of the crowd told him right to his face that he was taking it on the fly. Trubee said that he didn't understand what the fellow was driving at. His friend flipped a butt over the railing of the porch and watched it until it stopped rolling down the asphalt. Then he said that good little Trubee had picked a slick time for getting married; it was a smart way of ducking out of the draft. Before Trubee had a chance to say anything to that, the whole crowd walked away, leaving him alone on the porch of the Post Office.

Forgetting about the things that he'd come to the village to buy, forgetting about the wagon that he'd left tied up behind the Adirondack Inn, Trubee walked slowly down the highway until he reached the Schroon River bridge. On the way, he'd thought of what his friend had said to him, of how all his friends had acted, and now, as he looked down at the fastmoving water, he realized that he'd been a fool to listen to his father, that he'd had no damned business in the world to get married at a time like that. Everybody in Warrensburg was probably saying the same thing—that Trubee Pell, good little Trubee, good little Trubee, was taking it on the fly because he was ascared of going to war. Good little Trubee!

Under his feet the wooden timbers began to tremble as a car crossed the bridge, and idly he watched the jigging of loose sandgrains that lay on the planking. He raised his head when the driver of the car hailed him and asked for the way to Glens Falls and Albany. Trubee stared at him for a moment and then said that he'd point out the road; he was headed for Albany, too. The man snapped a door open and told Trubee to hop in; he always liked company when he was driving, he said.

At Albany, Trubee enlisted in the army. He wrote to no one during all the time he was in training, and no one knew where he was, but shortly before his regiment left for Hoboken he got leave to go home and say goodbye to his people. He went as far as Lake George. From there he telephoned to his wife and told her that he wanted to see her, but he warned her that if she brought his father along he wouldn't talk to either of them. Esther came down alone from Thurman an hour later. When Trubee met her at the bus stop, he said that he had to report back by midnight of the following day, and that he could stay overnight with her, but that was all. They put up at a small hotel on the lakefront.

After supper, they went for a walk along the windy and uneven shore, but before they'd gone very far it began to snow and they had to turn back. Esther was tired and wanted to go upstairs, but Trubee said that there was so much to be talked over that it'd be better if they stayed in the parlor and sat around the warm stove. After waiting almost an hour for the hotelkeeper to finish his paper, during which time Trubee did nothing but look at the flames behind the little windows of the grate, Esther got up and said good night. Trubee answered her, but kept on staring at the three red squares of mica before him. He listened, though, and over the rattling of the hotelkeeper's newspaper he heard his wife climb the stairs and close the door of their room behind her. For a long time he sat where he was, thinking only of what had happened in front of the Post Office the day of his marriage, but finally, with the fire dying and the parlor turning cold, he followed his wife to the bedroom. A small lamp was burning on the dresser. Esther was in bed, but she was still awake. Trubee sat down next to her.

She put her arms around him and told him that she loved him. He made her let go. He said that he was sorry, but he didn't love her; he thought she was a fine girl, the finest he'd ever met, but he didn't love her. In marrying her he'd done the wrong thing, he said, and he wanted her to divorce him after he went away. Then he told her what'd happened the day of the wedding, how his friends had turned their backs on him and walked away because they didn't want to have anything to do with a man who was so yellow that he had to hide behind a woman's apron. He said that he'd never feel right about their marriage and insisted that Esther do something to break it up. She tried to get near him again, but he wouldn't stand for it. In the end, she promised to do as he'd asked. They slept together that night, but only because there wasn't more than one bed in the room. Long before coming up to Lake George, Trubee had made up his mind what he was going to do, and he stuck to his decision.

Esther was the only one at the station to see him off. She cried when they said goodbye, and she was still crying when Trubee saw the last of her from the rear platform of the train. Then he cried, too, but by that time the station was no longer in sight.

A few months after he got to France he had a letter from Esther on the stationery of a lawyer from Saratoga; she told him that she was keeping her promise. Trubee didn't answer the letter, but that night, while he was off on a few hours' leave, he drank himself stupid and hooked up with a fat old ruin. He left with her all of his father's lessons, in return for which she gave him a dose of gonorrhea.

When Trubee came back to America, he had very shaky hands. They didn't flop around as if he had palsy, but they quivered, vibrated from side to side, blurred his fingers into one another until cigarette smoke rose above them in a scalloped column, until they seemed to expand like a telegraph wire that'd been hit by a stone. None of his friends liked to sleep with him. They said he kept them awake by shaking the bed, not much, not violently, but enough to make them think they were lying on a bench on the platform of a subway station.

The three men were James Pilgrim, Martin Flood, and Trubee Pell.

A few customers came into the saloon, took their drinks standing at the bar, talked to the bartender for a while, and then went out. It was nearly one o'clock. When Pilgrim, Flood, and Pell were again the only ones in the place, the bartender went over to their table and stood there without saying anything.

Flood looked up at him. "What do you want?" he said. "What are you standing around for?"

"It's getting late," the bartender said. "I'm closing up now."

The three men kept on talking.

The bartender went in between Pilgrim and Flood and started mopping off the table. "I guess you mugs didn't hear me," he said. "I'm closing up now. Beat it."

Flood said, "Go 'way, will you?"

The bartender picked up the three glasses and said, "The drinks come to three bucks. Kick in, and blow. I'm telling you again it's closing time."

Flood said, "It's closing time for *you*. Shut your face and go 'way from here." He looked down and started talking to his friends again.

The bartender said, "What's that you say, you tramp? Pay up for them drinks, or I'll kick the three of you out on your cans." He put the glasses back on the table.

Flood stood up slowly. He stood right against the bartender. "Kick who?" he said. "Get back behind that bar before I slap your puss in."

The bartender said, "You owe me three bucks."

Trubee held Flood's arm as it started up from the level of the table. He was almost pulled out of his chair. "Take it easy, Martin," he said. "Let's pay the bastard and get to Hell out of here." He pulled a dollarbill out of his pocket and offered it to the bartender, saying, "It's all we got."

When the bartender reached for the money, Flood batted his hand away. "For being such a fresh guy, you don't get paid," he said. He turned away and went to the door. Pilgrim and Pell followed him.

The three men crossed West Street and sat down on an empty packingcase that lay in the gutter near one of the dark piers, Flood and Pilgrim watching the doorway of the saloon and Trubee behind them looking at the scattered lights moving on the riverwater.

When the bartender came out of the saloon, glancing both ways before hurrying off toward the Chambers Street elevated station, Flood said, "I got a good mind to go over there and let that guy have it right between the eyes. And Trubee wanted to pay him, too. Let's take that bill and flop somewheres."

Trubee said, "First let's make up where we head for in the morning."

Pilgrim said, "I'd take you to some of the joints I used to know, but I don't stand in so good around here no more, not since I stuck up that crap game I was telling you about."

Flood said, "For Christ's sake, Turd, shut that hole of yours. All that comes out of it is gas. A fat lot of good you are. I say we should go down south. It's still too damned cold around here to suit me."

"I don't care one way or the other," Trubee said. "I got no place calling on me."

Flood said, "We start out tomorrow. Give me that bill, now, and we'll find out where there's a twobit hotel."

Trubee felt in his pockets, but couldn't find the bill. "Damn it, Martin," he said, "I must of dropped it back there in the saloon."

Flood stood up, slowly again, just as he'd done alongside of the bartender, and went over to where Trubee was sitting. He put his hand on Trubee's forearm, his fingers making a circle around it. "So you give that money away," he said without raising his voice. "And I told that sonofabitch he wasn't going to get paid."

"I didn't pay him, Martin. I lost the money, I tell you."

"Sure you lost it," Flood said. "Accidentally on purpose you lost it."

He hit Trubee a stinger on the side of the jaw, and Trubee fell off the packingcase and lay in the street with his eyes closed. After a moment he opened them and sat up, shaking his head a few times. He asked Pilgrim for a cigarette.

"That dough belonged to the three of us," Flood said.

Trubee rocked a little when he stood up. Leaning against the case for support, he reached for a halfsmoked butt that Pilgrim was holding out to him. He took a few drags on it.

Flood said, "That dough belonged to the three of us, and you didn't have no call to be giving it away."

"That's the Hudson out there," Trubee said, staring at a wedge of the broad dark river between two piers, "only it looks a whole lot different 'way down here."

"You talking about the river don't make me forget you give away our bedmoney," Flood said.

"You don't see any ships up there—some flatbottom row-boats, maybe, but that's all."

"Up where?"

"Up the river, up where she starts in, some place in the Newcomb country back of Long Lake."

"God damn it, Trubee!" Flood said. "Do I have to knock some more sense into that conk of yours? What the Hell you talking about scenery for when here we are without no place to sleep?"

"I'll take you to a place," Trubee said.

"*You'll* take!" Pilgrim said. "What do *you* know about this burg?"

Flood said, "Hold your horses, Turd. Where you going to take us, Trubee?"

"I can't take you tonight. It's too far."

"What's too far?"

"The place I'm talking about."

"Well, where in Hell is it? And who owns it?"

"I'm talking about my father's farm," Trubee said.

Flood said, "Only last week you was telling us you didn't never want to see the farm again. And you said you didn't never want to see your old man neither."

"I changed my mind."

"You changed it mighty quick. What's the idea?"

"I was thinking about it all the time we was in the saloon," Trubee said. "I was thinking maybe we should all go up and make a little social call on the old man."

Pilgrim said, "What do you mean—social?"

"I mean now I'm back in the country I shouldn't be so strange. Maybe the old man's been feeling low." He looked at Flood. Then he looked at Pilgrim.

Pilgrim began to smile. In the dark, the cracked tiles of his mouth were invisible. The smile made a hole in his face. "I get you, Trubee, I get you."

Trubee looked along the flat faces of the piers. He said, "He's going to be mighty glad to see us three, the old man is. It's dutiful of me to be thinking of him, and he's sure the one to appreciate it."

"I'll go any place I don't have to work," Flood said. "How far away is it?"

"About two hundred and fifty miles upstate. Maybe a little less."

"Think we can bum it in a day?" Flood said.

"What's the matter with us going in style?" Pilgrim said. "I mean on a train."

Flood said, "Christ, where do we get the money to be riding on a train?"

"Why not roll somebody?" Pilgrim said.

"Who?"

"One of them wop fruitdealers from over Avenue A. They drive to market around three in the morning, and they bring cash. We can nail one on the way and take him for what he's got. It's an old trick. I got away with it fourfive times."

"And a couple of times you didn't. Maybe you liked it up there in the pen, but me I'm not the kind to be setting around on my can for a couple of years just because I was hard up for some lousy money."

"I never got nabbed for this stunt," Pilgrim said, "and many's the time I worked it all alone. Here's three of us. The dago wouldn't have a chance."

When the others finally agreed to the plan, Pilgrim led the way up West Street for almost two miles, past the freight docks below 14th Street and then the long piers of the Cunard and White Star Lines. The waterfront was quiet and dark except at the docks where a ship was being loaded, and there dozens of drays and trucks crossed the carpets of yellow light that lay on the uneven cobblestones. The three men cut into 11th Avenue and followed it until they were only a few blocks from the 30th Street yards of the New York Central. They stopped in the doorway of a loft building while Pilgrim went hunting for something among the rubbish heaps of an empty lot. He was back in a couple of minutes with the broken leg of an iron bed, a piece of enameled pipe a little over a foot long; the end of it was wrapped in a burlap bag. They went around the corner of 27th Street and hid in an alley between 10th and 11th Avenues.

"This better be good, Turd," Flood said, "because if we get grabbed for it, you might just as well hang yourself while we're in the can."

"Quit worrying," Pilgrim said. "I know what I'm doing."

He told the others that when he gave them the tip, either Trubee or Flood was to step out onto the sidewalk and ask for a light from the driver of the wagon that was coming along; he said that he'd do the rest. Then, leaving them, he went directly across the street and disappeared in the driveway of a small factory.

During the next half hour, not a truck or a motorcar went by, but then Trubee heard the faraway creaking of wheels, the retching of dry wooden spokes, the plodding of hoofs on the asphalt. He stuck his head out a little and saw a wagon passing an arclight near the middle of the block. A low whistle sounded from across the gutter, and Trubee went out to the curb with a cold cigarette hanging from his mouth. When the wagon was in front of him, he asked the driver for a match.

"To Hella with you," the driver said, and grabbing his whip, he let his horse have a sharp one over its rump.

Instead of breaking into a run, the animal reared up as if a nail had been driven into it. Trubee got his foot on the step of the wagon, but as he started to climb up, the man turned the whip on him and almost cut his ear off with a good hard slash. Trubee held on because he saw Pilgrim coming out of the driveway. Thinking that Trubee was alone, the driver again tried to slice him loose and get away, but while he was giving all of his attention to the man on his left, Pilgrim reached up over the other side of the seat, hit him on the top of his skull with the piece of pipe, and laid him out cold in the bottom of the wagon. Then Flood came running out of the alley, and it took him only a second to lift the driver's purse. As soon as he had it, all three lit out for 10th Avenue. When they got there, they walked up to 28th Street, cut in east, and started running again. They ran as far as the 9th Avenue elevated, and then they took their time, zigzagging all the way across town to Park Avenue. At Grand Central they went down to the Men's Room. Finding nobody there, they opened the purse, took out the forty dollars it held, and then chucked the empty leather bag behind one of the toilets.

After a good feed at one of the station restaurants, they got a Red Cap to buy them three quarts of whisky. Around six o'clock in the morning they caught the Mohawk, a Buffalo express carrying a coach for Lake George.

CHAPTER TWO

Trubee woke up in Albany when the Delaware & Hudson car was dropped by the westbound and shunted off on a siding to be picked up by the Lake George local. All the way from Grand Central to the Marble Hill bend, he'd been thinking of nothing but how the river would look in the early sunlight; he'd fallen asleep when the flyer went through the Spuyten Duyvil cut and straightened out for the run to Harmon.

Looking around him now, he saw Flood sprawled out over a pair of seats. Right behind him, Pilgrim slept with one side of his face mashed flat against the windowpane. His mouth was open and limp, showing his rotted teeth. A sabre of hair drooped between his eyes. He swallowed, and his ears flirted up and down, once each way.

A switchengine came slowly up the track with a brakeman standing on the step of its sawedoff cowcatcher and revolving his hand on the axle of his wrist. The locomotive bunted the car out to the main line, where it was coupled with the last car of the local. The train pulled into the Albany station, and ten minutes later it left for Lake George.

Trubee drank what was left of his whisky, about a tumblerful, and taking the empty bottle, he went out to the rear platform of the car and stuck his elbows into the notches of the iron gate. Leaning against it, he stared at the track shooting out from under him and then at the shaking bottle he held loosely in his fingers. He stayed there that way for a long time. The bottle dropped out of his hand and smashed to pieces on the ties. He watched the shining hunks of glass until they disappeared into the waves of hot air that tumbled over the ballast.

Cohoes, Waterford, Mechanicville, Schuylerville. Trubee didn't know the country very well, but he'd been through it with his father a few times many years before. He remembered his tenth birthday, when he'd been taken on a trip to the Saratoga battlefields. He remembered the Blockhouse on top of a long-sweeping hill in the middle of a plain; he remembered the metal markers that were stuck all over the plain to show where the officers had fallen during the fight. He remembered having felt that the battle hadn't been fought so long ago; it'd seemed then that he was walking through the fields only the day after Burgoyne had been beaten.

Flood and Pilgrim were still asleep when, around noontime, the train started down the long grade toward the foot of Lake George. Trubee opened a window and leaned outside to watch the cars coast in for the buffers. The last time he'd seen the station, the train was going the other way. He remembered Esther on the platform. He remembered how she'd walked and then run with the last car all the way to the end of the sheds, where the train had put on steam to make the rise. He remembered Esther's face, and he remembered the look she'd given him the night before when he'd pushed her away from him in the hotel room.

There was no one on the platform now except a man wheeling a handtruck alongside of the baggage car. After getting something to eat in a lunchwagon on the main street of Lake George, the three men walked up to the north end of the town and waited for a ride at the Ticonderoga fork. A truck stopped for them in a little while. On the way to Warrensburg, the driver opened a bottle and took a pull at it; he sold the rest for a dollar, and Trubee drank most of it before they'd reached the Schroon River bridge.

They got off there, and after the truck had gone out of sight, Trubee pointed to a path going up a steep hill on the west side of the road. He told the others that the path went up the back of Harrington Hill and came out into the Viele Pond road just beyond the last farm on the way to his father's place; he said that the reason he was taking them across country was that it was shorter.

The climb up the path was almost three miles long, and Pilgrim fell down twice before they'd covered half the distance. The second time, while lying flat on his belly, he'd said he was thirsty and refused to budge until somebody got him a drink of water. When Flood planted a boot in his backside, he'd managed to get up without the water.

A few hundred yards past the junction of the path and the road to the Pond, they reached a small v in the sheer bank of red clay that rose on their left. In the crotch of this v lay a thin pipe, and from this a spill of water curved into a fat wooden barrel. Pilgrim flopped down on his knees alongside of the barrel and began to suck up a long drink, the water sounding as if it were going down a drain. Flood and Trubee drank from the end of the pipe.

The going was easier for the next two miles. Nothing seemed to have changed since Trubee's last ride down the road the morning of his marriage. From the shoulder of Harrington Hill the view was the same—the same slatecolored ridges in the north, the same cauliflower clouds slitting their bellies on the blades of Marcy and Whiteface. The same trees and bushes were beginning to blossom, their thin brightgreen leaves moving like ribbons on the branches or spinning in the wind like butterflies. The ground was papered brown with last year's leaves, and on both sides of the road greenspeckled boulders were scattered through the deep woods. In the hollows, the air smelled of still-damp leaves.

Pilgrim fell down again near the Viele Pond lodge, and this time he was unable to get up alone. Trubee and Flood took him by the arms and dragged him as far as a tree that stood close to the porch of the lodge. They leaned him against it, and then

Trubee went around to the rear of the boardedup house to get some water from the well.

Seeing the Pond through its picket of birches, Trubee climbed down the slope and broke through the briers until he was standing at the water's edge. The Pond was about a quarter of a mile long and a little less than that across its greatest width. The water lilies weren't open yet, but later on in the year there'd be a broad rim of cream spreading from the banks toward the center; when the lilies were in flower, the Pond would seem to be only half its size. Because of the depth, the middle water was always open; in some places, there were springholes that Trubee had never been able to plumb. On the east side of the Pond was a bad marsh filled with waterbushes, rotted trees, and jagged gray stumps. There were several nests of heron among the trees still standing, and sometimes the birds came down into the shallow water of the marsh and hunted for food by keeping as still as a fallen branch until something swam into sight. Going down the bank a little way, Trubee saw that the old beaver dam at the south end of the Pond had again been torn apart; he'd helped Harry Reoux to repair it a few summers before, but a recent thaw had finished it completely. The water that fell over the ruins of the dam made Stewart Brook, a fast run that foamed down over a stairway of green boulders. Breaking the steps in some places, there were deep gravel-bottomed troutpools almost hidden under the trees that came together over the water.

Hearing Flood's call, Trubee went back to the well. He found an old bucket lying under some bushes and lowered it at the end of a length of rope that was tied to the cover of the well. Carrying the water around to the front of the lodge, he found Flood looking down at Pilgrim, who was lying on the ground bleeding from a gash in his scalp.

"Smack him for something, Martin?"

"No. He just fell over."

When Trubee dumped some of the water on him, Pilgrim sat up and began to lick the drops off his hands. Then he buried his head in the pail and drank all he could hold.

After resting for a while, they started down the hill toward the Pell farm. For a mile and a half the road ran parallel to Stewart Brook, dropping with it over long slabs of outcropping shale to the bottom of a small valley. The stream broadened on the flat and flowed quickly around smooth knobs of rock for a short distance. Then it bent sharply under the road. The farm, hidden behind a cape of trees, began at the far side of the narrow plank bridge that lay across the creek.

An entire side of the farmhouse was gone, exposing two rooms, one above the other. The upper room was empty, but on the crumbling floor of the lower one were the rusted skeleton of a bed, a few broken chairs, a pile of warped shingles, and a heap of assorted junk. The inner side of these rooms was now the wall of the house. Loose paper and plaster bulged away from the laths. In some places, the plaster had come off in patches, and the holes were covered with bleached tarpaper that was held down by slats that'd been nailed across it. The roof of the house had been repaired in the same way, and where even the tarpaper had given out, there were sheets of tin made out of flattened gasoline cans. A few panes of glass remained in some of the windows; where the glass was missing, the openings had been plugged with rags and cardboard. A fence had fallen in on the yard, which was high with trash and overgrown weeds. Near the sagging porch, yellow stuffing boiled out of the cracked remains of an old Morris chair. At the base of the house, where once there'd been vines and flowerbushes, now there were only piles of broken crockery and mildewed newspaper, and a mound of tin cans red with rust. Alongside of the porch stood a farmwagon, missing the rear pair of wheels.

When Flood walked into the yard, he let go of Pilgrim, who fell facedown on the bulbs of a stale horseturd and went to sleep. Flood sat on the cracked tongue of the old wagon and waited for Trubee to do something. Rolling a cigarette, Trubee came in from the roadway. His shaky hands were going faster than ever and spilling most of the tobaccograins off the paper. When the cigarette was made, he hung it off his under lip, and then he sat down on the stump of a tamarack, remembering how he and his father used to put bottlecaps on it and shoot at them with an old Winchester from the runway of the barn. The stump was all that was left of a row of trees that'd been planted by his grandfather. He heard a loud droning under him and knew that wasps had bored into the punk and made it their nest.

Flood watched Trubee.

Walter Pell came through the barn, shading his eyes to see who was sitting on the treestump. Then he rushed straight for Trubee; a few yards away from him he stopped and held out his arms. Trubee kept on staring at the wet brown end of the cigarette that he held in his fingers.

"Trubee!" the old man said.

Trubee took a last drag before turning completely away from the old man to flip the butt away. "Hello, pop," he said without looking at his father. "How you feeling?"

Pell went over and tried to put his arms around Trubee, but Trubee pushed them away.

"I said how was you feeling, pop."

"I guess I'm all right, son."

"We come up here to make a little social call. From the way you was standing there, it looked for a minute like you wasn't any too glad to see us. Say hello to my friends. That's Martin Flood over there on the wagon."

"Please to meet you," the old man said.

Flood nodded, but said nothing.

"And laying right over there, that's Turd Pilgrim." He went over to Pilgrim and shook him a few times. "Turd, I just introduced you to my old man. This is a social call. Where's your manners? Get up and shake hands."

Pilgrim picked himself up like a child just learning how to walk; his behind went up in the air first. He stuck his hand out at the old man and opened his face for a smile, showing his treegreen teeth.

The old man didn't shake hands, but said, "Please to meet you."

"Now everything's nice and sociable," Trubee said. "I'm beginning to feel right at home. There's nothing like a friendly call to put a man in spirits—not that we need any spirits, pop." He burst out laughing and rocked back and forth. "No, sir. We don't need any spirits. Want to know why, pop?"

The old man said that he had some work to do. He turned around and started walking back toward the fields.

"Wait a minute, pop," Trubee said.

The old man stopped. "What do you want, Trubee?"

"I want to tell you why we don't need any spirits."

"You're drunk," the old man said.

"Hell! And I thought I had a big surprise for you. I was just going to *tell* you we was drunk. I was going to say we didn't need any spirits because we was all drunk. Now you went and spoiled my surprise."

The old man turned away again.

"Go get us something to eat!" Flood said.

Pell looked back at him. "Go get it yourself," he said.

Flood stood up. "Go get us something to eat, old timer." He went up to the old man and took him by the arm. "I said go get us something to eat."

Pell looked at Trubee, who was staring over the wagon at the trees on the far side of the road. "I got work to do," the old man said. "I got no time to be fooling around in the kitchen right now. If you want to eat, you'll find all the stuff in there."

Flood gave him a shove. "Get in that kitchen and fix us up a meal, unless you want me to haul you in there by your heels. After a trip like we just had, do you think I'm going to play around with a stove? What in Hell do you take me for, anyway? Are you going in, or do I have to make you?"

Trubee was still staring at the trees.

"All right," the old man said to Flood. "I'll see what I can do for you."

"Make it fast," Flood said. Then he went back to the wagon-tongue and sat down again.

When the old man neared the kitchen, he heard Trubee say, "Now, that's what I call mighty sociable of the old guy."

CHAPTER THREE

While his father was preparing the meal, Trubee walked back to the barn and took a look at the fields. He saw there no sign of the disrepair that made the farmhouse seem as if it'd been abandoned for many years. A trim yard ran all the way from the door of the kitchen to the barn. The farm equipment was still in fair condition, and the stalls in the barn were clean, and they smelled of the sticks of straw that drifted down from the stuffed lofts. Through the back door, which opened into a good pasture, four fat Jerseys were grazing, and in a corner of the same field, two workhorses stood under a tree out of the warmth of a late April sun. To the left of the pasture there was a broad fallow field of clover in leaf, and beyond that were the vegetable rows. The orchard was on the other side of the pasture. Each of the apple and pear trees made a bright ball of new leaf, and under them were neat brown whirlpools of plowed ground.

When Trubee returned to the house, he found his friends seated at the table in the kitchen. In front of them were a platter of fried eggs and potatoes, a pot of coffee, and a loaf of bread. Pilgrim had torn a hunk off the bread, and he was ramming it into his face.

Flood looked at the food and then at the old man. "Where's the meat?" he said.

"There's none in the house except the heel of a ham."

"Bring it out," Flood said, "and bring some butter and milk, too. This is a Hell of a way to be setting a table. You'd think we was still in the God damned army."

"The ham's kind of old."

"Let it be old. It's meat, ain't it?"

"It's not much good any more."

"Go get it!"

When the old man came back with the meat, Flood put his head down and took a few sniffs at it. Then he grabbed it off the plate and pitched it at the old man's head. It hit the wall behind him, bounced off, and landed on a chair.

"Take that lousy garbage out of here," Flood said. "It stinks out loud. Is that all the meat you got?"

"Yes," Pell said.

Flood took a plateful of eggs and potatoes. "These eggs won't fill up the hole I got in my gut. I'm not in the God damned army any more, thank Christ. How about them chickens out in the yard?"

Trubee said, "Don't worry about meat, Martin. I know how to get some right off."

"So do I," Flood said. "All I got to do is catch hold of a hen and wring its skinny little neck."

Trubee said, "To Hell with chicken. I'll take you out tonight to a place I know, and if we have any luck we'll get enough meat to choke ourselves on."

Walter Pell was the only one who didn't eat; he just sat there at the table, staring at Trubee. Nobody talked to him during the meal; nobody even looked his way. When Trubee and his friends were finished, they rolled cigarettes, lit them, and got up to leave the room.

"Fix the dishes, pop," Trubee said from the doorway. "Flood and me, we got something to do. Where do you keep the guns?"

"Where you left them," the old man said. "In the parlor closet."

"Any shells and cartridges?"

"They're in the closet, too."

There were two shotguns and two rifles. The shotguns were doublebarreled 12 gauges. One of the rifles was Trubee's light Winchester, and the other was a leveraction 30.30. Only the Winchester had been kept in condition. Trubee got some ramrods, rags, and oil, and then he and Flood went out behind the barn with the other three guns. Flood worked on the 30.30 while Trubee took care of the shotguns, and in half an hour's time they had them clean enough for use. After Trubee had gotten a few shells and cartridges from the house, they tested the guns. Flood called off a dark smear on a grayish pole that stood out clearly against the dark green of the woods. He fired three shots at it with the 30.30.

"It shoots pretty good," he said as they crossed the field to see how he'd made out. "Not much kick. I think I made some hits."

There were two holes touching the knot, and one a couple of inches below it.

"Not bad shooting," Trubee said. "Why didn't you show some of that in France? You'd of come back wearing a medal."

"I'm no sucker. If I'd of let on I knowed which end of the gun the bullets came out of, they'd of stuck me up in a tree and made a sniper out of me. That target practice was just to see which of the guys was sappy enough to be begging them for permission to get conked in a hurry."

Trubee tried the shotguns against a claybank. One of them almost knocked him flat when he pulled the trigger.

"Jesus," he said. "It went into me like a plowhandle when you turn up a rock. I'm leaving that one home."

Flood said, "I wish the Turd knowed something about the woods. If he did, I wouldn't have to be going out. This breaks my rule about work. What time do we start?"

"Not before eleven."

"Then how about you and me corking off for a few hours?"

"All right, but first get the Turd to wake us up at the right time. Then I'll show you where we bunk. Give me the gun."

While Flood was telling Pilgrim what to do, Trubee went back to the closet and got out half a dozen shotgun shells and a handful of cartridges, putting them in a corner of the parlor with a couple of heavy shirts that he dug out of a trunk. Then he went out to the barn again and took the carbide lamp off an old buggy. He fixed the lamp so that it'd throw a wide beam, and put it in the parlor along with the shirts. When Flood came in, Trubee started to lead the way upstairs.

Old man Pell stopped them, saying that he wanted to talk to Trubee.

Trubee looked down the staircase and said, "What's on your mind?"

"Come down a minute," the old man said. "I want to talk to you."

"What about? Can't you say it from there?"

"No. It's something private."

Flood went up alone.

"Come in the parlor, Trubee," the old man said.

Trubee went down again and followed his father. The old man took a seat at the table and motioned to Trubee to sit down opposite him. Trubee went over to one side of the room and sat on a stool in front of an old melodeon that'd belonged to his mother.

The old man said, "This is the first chance I've had to talk to you since you come home."

"What do you want to talk about?" Trubee said. "I don't see where there's so much to say."

"I thought maybe you'd be wanting to hear about Esther."

Trubee got up from the stool. "Did you?" he said. *"Did you?"* Then he turned his back on the old man and walked out of the room.

Upstairs, he took Flood into a large bedroom at the front of the house. It was the one his father slept in, and it had a double bed. Trubee collected the old man's stuff and put it out in the hall, and he and Flood were getting undressed when Pell came up to the room and saw his things lying on the floor outside.

"I wasn't expecting you to stay in this room," he said.

"Why not?" Trubee said.

"You ought to know how I feel about that."

"How you feel about what?"

"About this room. I'm the only one has stayed here since your ma died."

"That's a long time ago. What's it got to do with us sleeping here now?"

"It's not the right thing. Use your own room in back."

"Don't kid me," Trubee said. "Sleep in there yourself."

The old man looked at him for a couple of seconds. Then he picked up an armful of his clothes and started to come into the room.

Trubee jumped off the bed and stood in the old man's way. "Get to Hell out of here," he said. "It's time you got wise that I'm the boss around this place." Then he shoved the old man out of the bedroom and slammed the door in his face.

As they got into bed, Flood said, "Good boy, Trubee." After that he was quiet for a while. Then he sat halfway up, leaning on his elbow and looking down at Trubee. "Except that part about who's boss," he said. "You don't mean that you're boss over me, do you?"

Trubee didn't answer.

"Do you hear me, Trubee? You don't mean that you're the boss when I'm around, do you?"

"I heard you, Martin. Let's get some sleep."

Flood lay back again and looked at the ceiling. He laughed without making a sound. Then he said, "Don't shake the bed too much with them lousy hands of yours. That's an order."

In a little while they heard the old man taking his stuff away from the door. Then they fell asleep.

Pilgrim woke them up at eleven o'clock that night. "Turn out, you guys," he said. "I want a crack at that hay."

It was very cold when they tossed back the blankets and got out of bed. In the light of the lamp that Pilgrim had brought with him, they could see their breath hanging before their faces for a second like pale blue smoke. The water in the pitcher on the washstand was covered by a thin lid of ice. Dressing themselves, Trubee and Flood went downstairs and put the heavy shirts on over their jackets. Flood took the rifle, and Trubee the shotgun and the lamp, and then they left the house.

Pilgrim followed them as far as the doorway. "For Christ's sake," he said, "come back with something, even if it's only a weasel."

They were crossing the yard and making for the road when Trubee spotted a figure standing between the gateposts.

"Who's that?" he called out.

"It's me, Trubee," his father said.

"God damn it, you throwed a scare into me! I was thinking it might be the gamewarden."

"Where you going, Trubee?"

"What the Hell's the big idea of sneaking around in the dark like that? Why don't you go to bed where you belong?"

"Where you going, Trubee?"

"One side, farmer," Flood said. "We're in a hurry."

With the rifle slung under his arm like a lance, but carelessly, as if he'd forgotten that he was carrying it, Flood moved forward; the muzzle of the gun was pointed straight at the old man's belly. Flood stopped when he felt the tip of the barrel sink into Pell's flesh.

"They caught a man over to Stony Creek last month," the old man said, "and they fined him a hundred dollars. I don't have any money to be paying your fines with, Trubee."

"One side, farmer, one side," Flood said, shoving Pell out of his way with the rifle. "Come on, Trubee."

They crossed the road and went through a damp meadow to a fence that ran along the edge of the woods. Following the fence until it angled back toward the road, they cut into the brush and went up the bed of a dried creek for a couple of miles over rocks and fallen trees. When they reached the head of the creek, they were in a valley filled with young timber. Trubee led the way through this to a smaller valley that opened off it and came to an end against the side of a sharpsloping mountain, at the foot of which there was a small marsh surrounded by boulders and underbrush. Trubee set the jacklight on a flat rock close to the marsh. After he and Flood had taken places on opposite sides of the rock, he lit the lamp and pointed the beam at a corner of the body of water. He took the safe off the shotgun, and Flood cocked the hammer of the rifle, and then both of them leaned against the rock and waited.

For more than an hour, they hardly made a move, and neither of them said a word. The woods were full of small sounds: the blurt of bullfrogs in the marsh; the bubbling of water; and, once in a while, from far off, the snapping of a stick of wood. On the other side of the swamp a woodthrush made its call, a short series of clearly fluted notes, and behind the men, but further away, another thrush answered. Occasionally a hoot owl sounded off, and three times they heard the distant baying of a dog.

Their flesh froze as tight as cold leather when they heard a sharp crack from the far side of the water, not a hundred feet away.

Very slowly and quietly they raised their guns and sighted down the wedge of light. There was a low brushing among the leaves and branches near the marsh; if it hadn't been for the cracking of the branch, the men would have thought that the sound had been made by the wind. The brushing stopped and then started again, this time a little nearer the right edge of the light. Trubee and Flood sat tight against the rock and peered down the lightcone for a moving form.

A large doe stepped out of the darkness, standing full in the lampline with her head held high. She looked right into the eye of the jacklight.

Trubee and Flood fired almost together, the explosions bouncing off the hills four or five times before dying away. The doe went down on one knee, but bucked to her feet again and turned to run with one leg dragging. As she swung, Trubee let her have the second barrel flush in the side, and Flood let go another slug that went wild. Then both men jumped up and dashed for the place where the deer had swerved into the dark. She hadn't gone ten feet, and was done for. She was down, with both legs buckled under her, and she was breathing very hard. As she started to go over, she made a last effort to get up and run; her strength was gone, and she went over on her flank. In a few seconds, she was dead.

The men took off their belts, and each bound up a pair of the deer's legs. They slid a branch through the belts and hoisted the load up to their shoulders. Trubee took the front end and stopped at the other side of the marsh to pick up the lamp and guns.

The trip back took a long time. Keeping to the woods for the entire distance, they neither heard nor saw anybody along the way. They had to rest several times even though they were in a hurry to get back to the farm and put the meat out of sight, and it was morning, almost six o'clock, before they reached the meadow across the road from the house. Trubee told Flood to stay at the edge of the trees while he went ahead for a look up and down the road. Seeing nothing, he ran back to where he'd left Flood, and then they quickly carried the deer around to the kitchen.

Trubee found a roll of muslin in the trunk, and they wrapped the cloth around the deer, leaving no part of it exposed to the blowflies except the hoofs. Then Trubee took the load down to the cellar and hung it from a hook that was screwed into one of the crossbeams.

After this, he and Flood went upstairs, and Flood turned
Pilgrim out of bed. Pilgrim kicked a little and wanted to know
where he was going to sleep for the rest of the night. Trubee told
him that he'd find a cot up in the attic.

Trubee woke up a little after five o'clock that afternoon. It
took some arguing to get Flood out from under the covers, but
finally both of them went down to the kitchen. Pilgrim had been
downstairs for a few hours, and was waiting for them. They had
something to eat, and then they got to work on the deer. All Flood
would do was help Pilgrim lug the carcass up from the cellar and
hang it by its forelegs from a stout maple behind the barn; after
that, he sat down in the sun and watched the others. Pilgrim was
so useless that Trubee told him to sit down, too.

Trubee honed a fourinch jackknife for several minutes, and
when it was sharp enough, he jammed the blade into where the
deer's neck joined its back. Then he cut the hide in a circle around
the neck and ran the blade from the withers down over the shoulders to the breastpoint on each side. Sticking the knife into the
skin over the first stomach, he slashed up along the middle of
the chest to meet the cut in the neckcircle. After that, using the
knife the other way from the cut in the stomach, he slit the hide
back to the end of the tail. The next cuts were on the inner side
of each leg, from the hoof to the gash in the belly. Then he sawed
the knifeblade through the skin and muscle of the shanks and
snapped them off. When that'd been done, he started to peel off
the hide. He got Pilgrim to help him with this, and it was only a
little while before the carcass was stripped.

Working with the knife again, Trubee shoved it into the meat
along the breastbone and cut through all the way to the tip. After
opening the abdomen, he stretched it and had Pilgrim prop it
open with sticks. He cut out all the guts and then washed the
hole out with water. Pilgrim let the body down to the ground,
and Trubee chopped the head off with an axe. Using the axe and

a long kitchenknife, he butchered the meat into steaks. He cut the liver out of the guts and told Pilgrim to get a spade and bury the rest. Then he carried the meat back to the house. Except for the liver and one large steak, he took all of it down to the cellar again, wrapped it in strips of the muslin, and hung the bundles from the crossbeam.

By the time he'd finished, old man Pell had come in from the fields. Trubee gave him the meat and told him to fry it along with some potatoes and onions. He also told him to open a couple of cans of beans and put up water for coffee, saying that they were all starved and that it'd be a good idea to see to it that there was enough to go around a few times.

Then Trubee and his friends went outside.

CHAPTER FOUR

After nightfall, Trubee and Flood started off down the road in the direction of Luzerne. Each of them carried a rifle, Flood the 30.30 again, and Trubee the old Winchester. Pilgrim spotted them leaving the house and ran after them to find out where they were bound for. When they heard him running, they stopped and waited for him to catch up to them.

"Where you going?" Pilgrim said.

"What's it *to* you?" Flood said. "If we'd of wanted you to come, we could of asked you. Now get back to the house and keep a tight hole in your face till we come back."

"I bet you guys is out for a good time," Pilgrim said. "What's a matter with me going along. I could use a good time just like anybody else."

Flood said, "That's all you think about is a good time."

Pilgrim let out a laugh. "And I suppose you're the kind that likes to stick around the Y. M. C. A. singing psalms. Sure you are—in a pig's brown."

"A good time means a whole lot more to me than it'll ever mean to you, but when I'm out looking for a party I don't have to carry no rifle to get the broad to feeling sociable. We don't happen to be looking for no piece tonight, so go back in the house and keep your conk closed except you want to get your brains all pounded into a jelly when I come back."

"The three of us is together. I got a right to know where you're headed."

"You got a right to do like I tell you. Now get to Hell out of here."

"All right, all right," Pilgrim said, "but what you getting so God damned high about? Who the Hell are you, anyway?"

Flood started for him, and the little man backed up a few yards.

"Maybe you want a bust in the jaw right now," Flood said. He turned around and asked Trubee to hold the rifle for him.

Instead of taking the rifle, Trubee slapped him on the arm. "Lay off, Martin," he said. "He don't want a bust in the jaw. He's just a little bit excited about the notion of a bust in the mouth. That's all his trouble." He started to laugh and kept it up until the others joined in with him. Afterward, Pilgrim went back to the house.

Trubee and Flood were out for whisky. They had no idea where they were going to get it without money, but Trubee had said that there was no telling what might turn up down at the state road. There'd been a lot of smuggling long before Prohibition came in, and he couldn't figure out why there shouldn't be some rumrunning now; as a matter of fact, according to the way he looked at it, most of the liquor that was sold by bootleggers in the States probably came in over the Canadian line. You couldn't stop a man from drinking just because you passed a law about it, and it was a sure thing that the stuff came from somewhere because there was just as much of it around after the law as there was before—and the odds were that that somewhere was Canada. He'd told Flood that it was his guess that the whisky came through in motor-trucks during the night, and that if everything broke right for them, there was a chance of their cutting in on some of it. In any case, they'd decided, they were going to have a whack at it. They knew a thing or two about guns, and if it came to a showdown, either with them or without them, they could handle themselves as well as the next man.

About a mile down, the road forked south and west. They took the west branch because there were fewer farms along it, and for a long time they walked toward the dim mass of Potash Mountain. They avoided the houses at the foot of it by cutting into the woods and coming out to the dirt again several hundred yards beyond the last field. From there to the Hudson River, there were no buildings of any kind. At the turn of the road stood a small white church, and behind this a catwalk footbridge crossed the shallow stream.

On the other side of the bridge, there was a narrow strip of timber between the water and the state road. The singletrack right of way of the Adirondack Railroad cut this in two. Beyond the rails, the trees were closely bunched up to the edge of the highway. No lights showed in either direction, north toward Stony Creek or south toward Hadley and Luzerne. Trubee and Flood hid themselves behind a fallen tree at the roadside and waited for something to happen. It was close to midnight.

Three or four cars and trucks passed during the next hour, but there was nothing about them to show that they were what the two men were looking for. Finally a touring car came around a bend going south at a pretty slow clip; its curtains were up, and a searchlight was being played from side to side into the woods. Ten minutes after it'd gone out of sight, a truck rounded the bend, and in five or six minutes a second truck followed. Trubee crawled up to the turn and looked down a long gradual straightaway; another truck was coming up the hill. When it'd passed, Trubee saw a fourth car starting up from the bottom of the grade.

Seeing no more of them coming, but still taking the long chance that this was the last of the trucks, he ran back to where Flood was hiding, and then both of them almost tore their arms out to get the dead tree across the pavement. They just had time to put rocks between themselves and the road before the lamps of the fourth truck showed at the curve. They heard the motor getting more gas for the level stretch, and then the truck made the turn. Fifty feet away from it, the tree was blocking the way. As soon as the driver spotted it, he yanked on his brakes and switched off the headlights. The truck stopped just short of the tree. For almost a minute, the idling motor made the only sound.

Then Trubee spoke up. He said, "Turn on them lamps and get out of the cab."

The motor was shut off, but the driver stayed where he was.

"You're covered six different ways," Trubee said, "and you got just about one minute to make up your mind if you want to come out."

At the end of that time, there was still no sound from the truck, so Flood and Trubee each put a shot over the top of the cab, and then, quickly changing their positions, they each fired again. After the second round, the lights of the truck were turned on.

A voice came through the windshield. "What the Hell do you want us to do?"

"Come out with your hands up and head straight for the front of the truck," Trubee said. "If you budge without you're told, you get some lead right square in the liver."

"You win, farmer," said the voice. "Here we come."

Two men jumped out into the road and, with their hands up in the air, went around to the front of the truck to stand in the line of the headlights.

"If there's anybody left in that cab, you better tell him to come out before he gets blowed out," Trubee said.

"Us two is the only ones."

"How do we know?"

"Come on out and take a look."

"O.K., but if somebody starts in getting gay, you two get mowed down first."

Flood leaned over a rock and covered the two men with the 30.30 while Trubee came out and took a look into the cab. Then he climbed up over the back of the truck to make sure that there was whisky in the cases under the canvas tarpaulin.

"Come on down, boys," he called. "We're up to our knees in luck."

When Flood showed himself, and the rumrunners saw that they'd been jobbed by only two men, they began to swear blue murder.

"Luck is right," one of them said. "You rubes could flop head-first into a crapper and come up with a gold watch."

Trubee took the wheel. He backed the truck into a draw and then headed north in the direction of Stony Creek. They passed only one car on the way to the bridge at Thurman, a roadster traveling very fast. After Stony Creek, the road jogged to the northeast, following the river and the railroad. At Thurman, it crossed over and bent east toward Warrensburg. They passed the junction of the Schroon and the Hudson, and kept on going until they were in the outskirts of the village. Then they cut south into a onetrack dirt pike that joined the Viele Pond road about two miles from the lodge.

Trubee drove into the barn around four o'clock in the morning, and in the gray light that was beginning to show over the fields through the back door, he and Flood inspected their haul. Under the canvas, they found nearly two hundred cases of Johnnie Walker's Black Label Scotch. They broke open a couple of pints and took a few stiff pulls before settling down to serious work. They sat on the floor and drank leaning against the runningboard of the truck. In a little while, they found that it was easier to lie flat on the floor and pour the whisky down their throats. They didn't give a damn how much they wasted; they had enough alcohol on the truck to float a ferryboat. The whisky ran out of the corners of their mouths and down into their ears; they gargled with it, washed their faces in it, splashed it over their hair. Under their heads, there were pools of it on the worn planking of the floor. Their talk got louder and louder, and they began to throw bottles against the stalls. They banged their heels to keep time with all the verses of "Hinky Dinky Parlezvous" and "The Bastard King Of England."

The noise woke Pilgrim up, and he came down from the attic in his long heavy underwear to see what the trouble was. He barefooted it across the yard to the barndoor, looked around him for a second, and then ran for the tailboard of the truck, stubbing his toes on the head of a spike and cursing God and Hell until the pain went away. In the meantime, he pulled a pint of whisky out of the open case and tried to get the cork out with his fingers and then with his teeth. He worked so fast that the bottle slipped out of his hands and smashed to pieces against the hub of a wheel. He grabbed another bottle, and managing to get it open, he tilted the bottom up and drank off almost a third of the whisky before going over to congratulate his friends. They didn't even know that he was there.

After a while, Trubee fell asleep. Flood got as far as a horse-blanket near the wall. Pilgrim climbed up on the truck and passed out lying across the whisky cases.

CHAPTER FIVE

Pell found the three of them when he came through the barn later in the morning. He took Trubee by the shoulder and shook him until he woke up. Then he caught hold of Pilgrim's arm, which was hanging over the side of the truck, and pulled him down to the floor. With the little man came a fresh bottle of Johnnie Walker that he'd been holding since he fell asleep; the bottle bumped across the boards as Pell dragged him over to the wall and sat him down alongside of Trubee.

Both of them looked up at the old man, who was standing with his back to the great square of sunlight framed by the door of the barn. Trubee squinted for a few seconds, and then his eyes began to close. He saw the figure before him through the blazing bars of his eyelashes, and this frightened him into keeping his eyes open. He turned away and stared into the restful shadow of the stalls.

After kicking the empty bottles into a corner, Pell came back and stood before Trubee again. Disturbed by the rumbling of the bottles over the uneven planks, Flood sat up and yawned, showing a tongue that looked as if it were wrapped in gauze. He puckered his face and spat a blob of white foam into the air. It landed near the old man's feet. Flood climbed him in sections, his slowlifting eyes making brief stops at Pell's knees, belt, chest, and chin, before fixing on the chlorinatedwaterblue eyes that were looking down at him.

"Help yourself to a slug, pop," Trubee said.

"You drunkard!" the old man said.

"Pass him that bottle, Pilgrim. He needs a drink."

Pilgrim fiddled with the bottle like a monkey trying to wind up a mechanical toy. He couldn't seem to find out the right way to hold it, and finally it fell to the floor. Pilgrim looked up with an expression of exhausted surprise that turned suddenly into a quick grin and then faded.

"Get sociable, pop," Trubee said. "Come off of that high horse of yours and try some Johnnie Walker. Flood and me, we stole it last night."

"What in the name of God's come over you, Trubee? Why are you carrying on like this?"

"*Who's* carrying on? You mean *me*? You mean *I'm* carrying on?"

"I don't mean anybody else," the old man said. "I don't care about anybody else."

"Now, that's a fine way for you to be talking, and right in front of people that's visiting you. I don't call that being sociable at all."

"I don't care what you call it, but it's high time I put my foot down on this kind of nonsense. I didn't say nothing when you blew in here dead drunk the day before yesterday; I didn't say nothing when you brung along a couple of strangers with you; and I didn't say nothing even when you went around shooting up the woods and making yourself liable to a good stiff fine if they caught you taking a deer out of season; but I'll be hanged if I'm going to sit by and watch you drink yourself to death with these hoboes that you picked up God only knows where and why."

"Now, now, you shouldn't be saying things like that," Trubee said. "They're good friends of mine, and what's more, they just got finished being soldiers of the U. S. A. Maybe you don't know it, but they hung Kaiser Bill to a sour apple tree and made the world safe for democracy. Didn't you, boys?"

He turned to Flood and Pilgrim and let out the first few dadas of "The Stars And Stripes Forever." Flood came in with the bumbums of the French horn, and Pilgrim, with his high thin voice, did a comedy plinkplink in the pauses. They all kept time with their feet. When they were finished braying the song, Flood yanked the cork out of the bottle, took a long swig, and then handed the rest of the whisky over to his friends.

Holding the bottle in his hand, Trubee looked at his father again. "What was you saying a minute ago, pop?" he said.

"I was saying this, Trubee—that I don't want those bums hanging around my farm. They got to go, and that's all there is to it."

"Who's got to go, mister?" Flood said.

Pell turned to him. "You and that foxy little partner of yours—that's who. This is my farm, I'll have you to know, and it's always been a respectable place. There never was any drinking and bumming going on here, and there never will be. I don't care who you are, or how good a friend of Trubee's—you've got to get out of my house."

Flood looked at him, but said nothing.

"I hope you heard me, stranger," Pell said. "Git, and the sooner the better."

Still looking at the old man, Flood held out his hand for the whisky bottle. Trubee gave it to him.

Pell raised his voice for the first time. "I told you two to git, and I meant what I said. I don't want any truck with your kind, and I don't want my boy to have, neither. You're a couple of hoodlums—that's what you are—and you're going to run your heads into a heap of trouble if you don't make yourself scarce in a pretty big hurry. Making me cook meals for you! Sticking a rifle in my belly! Taking over a room that nobody but me has slept in since my wife died! Why, by God, I ought to take a whip to you, you lowlives! I want you to get out of here, I tell you. I want you to get out!"

Flood leaned back against the wall, raising the bottle to his mouth for another drink. While he was swallowing the mouthful, something struck him funny, and he suddenly ducked his head forward and sprayed out the whisky like an atomizer. Trubee watched the fineblown mist float in the air for a few seconds before it settled to the floor.

Pilgrim looked at Flood and said, "Hey, there, quit wasting that stuff."

"Couldn't help it," Flood said.

"I want you two to clear out of here," the old man said. "I stood just about enough from you loafers, and I'm all fed up. You don't belong here, and the quicker you get back to where you come from the better it'll suit me. I want you to leave me and my boy alone."

Flood started to tilt the bottle again, and this time, even before it reached his mouth, he clapped a hand to his throat and doubled up. A dry swallow had gotten stuck when it was halfway down, and it choked him until it turned into a sneeze. He smiled over the icicle of mucus that it spun from his nostrils, but after the twisting lavaliere had torn itself loose, he leaned back once more and touched off a burst of laughter.

Pilgrim laughed, too. "Plink, plink," he said. "What's the big joke, Martin?"

Flood laughed until he was sprawled out like a drowned man; once in a while, his body was twitched by the fingertips of a sneaking wave.

Pilgrim said, "Let me in on it, Martin. What's so funny?"

As he spoke, he looked at Flood, and then the two of them blew another laugh through the arbor of the barn. Pilgrim's part was the hysterical tenor of a child, and Flood's, although it started deep in the grotto of his throat, quickly mounted to the same pitch.

"What's the joke, Martin?" Pilgrim said as the gust was dying away.

The old man said, "This was always a respectable place, and I want you two...."

Renewed, the wind of Flood's laugh came back, and once more it echoed off the walls, catching up Pilgrim's shrill bleating again.

"Plink, plink," the little man tried to say before giving in to the laugh, but the sounds revolted far back in his throat and mobbed their way upward as if they were going to force an exit through the top of his skull. He drove them back with an exhalation and managed to get them out by way of his nostrils and lips. "Plink, plink," he said, and then he lay flat on the floor and laughed until the pain of pleasure made him grab his belly with both hands and squeeze it as if he had a cramp.

"For Christ's sake, Martin, spring the joke before I bust a gut."

The old man said, "This is a respectable place...."

"Plink, plink."

Trubee giggled.

Flood and Pilgrim acted as if this were all they'd been waiting to hear. Flood rolled off the horseblanket and lay facedown on the floor, beating his fists on the planks and laughing so hard that he bounced. Pilgrim went loose all over and let out a series of barking shrieks that sounded as if they were being punched out of a stuffed animal. Trubee's giggling came out in gurgles, like water being dumped from a narrownecked bottle. He raised his arms to conduct an encore of "The Stars And Stripes Forever."

"Da da dadada dadada," he said.

"Bum bum bumbumbum bumbumbum," Flood said.

"Plink plink plinkplinkplink plinkplinkplink," Pilgrim said.

The old man turned his back on them in the middle of the song. He went over to one of the stalls, backed a horse out, and led him to the front of the barn, where the wagon was standing. While the horse was being hitched, Trubee got up and walked over to the big sliding door. He stood there leaning against it and watching his father, who was busy buckling the harness.

"Where you going, pop?"

"Down to Warrensburg," the old man said, keeping on with what he was doing.

"What for?"

Pell nodded over Trubee's shoulder. "For that in there," he said.

Trubee looked back and saw that the two men were eyeing him.

"For that in there," the old man repeated.

"What do you expect to do about it in Warrensburg?"

"Ed Smead."

"So you're going to see the sheriff."

"You bet, son."

Flood and Pilgrim came walking out of the barn and stopped alongside of Trubee. Flood was carrying the bottle of whisky.

"What'll you gain by that?" Trubee said to his father.

"A little peace and quiet."

"How?"

"How? Why, I'm going to get Ed Smead to run them tramp friends of yours right out of the county—that's how."

"You don't want to do that, do you?"

"Don't I, son? Just watch me."

Pell climbed up to the wagonseat, wrapped the reins around his palms, and let out a cluck to the horse. The animal got under way.

Trubee called to his father. "When Flood and Pilgrim go, I go, too. I just thought I'd tell you."

Pell stopped the wagon and turned on the seat. "What do you mean by that?"

"Just what I said. It's plain enough. If you get Smead to put my friends out, I go along with them. And I don't ever come back. You can take your pick."

For several seconds the old man looked at him. Neither of them spoke. Then Pell turned slowly away, slapped the reins on the horse's rump, and drove out of the yard.

When the wagon was out of sight, Trubee said, "Let's have a drink, Martin."

"Now, what?" Flood said as he held out the bottle.

"Don't worry," Trubee said. "He didn't get to Warrensburg yet."

Pilgrim said, "Leave a couple of fingers for me, will you, Trubee? Say, Martin, what the Hell was we all laughing about before?"

They sat down in the shade of the barn, and none of them said anything for about a quarter of an hour. Then they heard the sound of the iron tires of the wagon scratching through the gravel.

Trubee looked at Flood. Both of them grinned.

"You didn't answer me before, Martin," Pilgrim said. "What was we all laughing about?"

Late that afternoon, the old man stopped the team at the end of a furrow and wiped the sweat off his face with one of his shirtsleeves. Then he hitched the reins a little higher under his arms and around his back, and he was about to take up the plow-handles again when he heard several shots from behind the barn. He didn't know what to make of the shooting at first, but he put two and two together when he heard the sound of breaking glass, and figured that Trubee and his friends were passing the time of day in some target practice.

Deciding to knock off for the day, Pell unhitched the horses from the plow and walked them along a path at the side of the field. As he neared the barn with the team, he heard another round of shots explode from the other side of the building. After putting the animals into their stalls and loading their feedboxes with a few measures of oats, he went outside to see whether Trubee and his friends were sober enough to listen to reason.

The three of them were on top of a haystack. Pilgrim was sitting up and keeping score; he had a piece of chalk in his hand and a couple of shingles across his knees. Trubee and Flood were lying on their bellies alongside of him and taking turns at firing the rifle. Just as the old man came out of the barn, Flood rolled over and handed the heavy Savage repeater to Trubee. Leaning on his elbows, the boy took the gun and squinted down the barrel. Even from where Pell was standing, he could see the muzzle rocking from side to side. For several seconds Trubee tried to steady himself, but the longer he aimed the more he shook. He changed his position a little and tried all over again. His fingers pressed the barrel and jammed the stock up against his shoulder, but from the way the gun kept on swinging around the old man knew that Trubee had more chance of hitting a fly on the wing than whatever it was he was aiming at. What was the target, anyway? Pell's eyes began to follow the line of the gun, but before he'd located the mark he heard Flood talking.

"Come on, shoot it off. What the Hell you waiting for?"

"It's moving," Trubee said.

"What's moving?"

"That God damned bottle."

Flood laughed. "You mean the haystack's moving, don't you? It's bucking under you like a horse. You better hold on or you'll get throwed off on your can."

"Joking aside," Trubee said. "That bottle's moving."

"Sure, and so's your hands. Why don't you own up?"

"Nothing to own up to. That bottle's moving. It's trying mighty hard to spoil my shot."

"God damn it!" Flood said. "Shoot that gun off or give up your turn."

"Give up! I don't never give up. When I start in to do something, I don't never give up. That's that Pell blood I got in me."

"Trouble with that Pell blood is that it's clogged up with wool."

"Wool, Hell! It's filled with bullets. You won't find any Indian knows more about shooting than the Pells. What we don't know about shooting ain't worth knowing."

"Let's see some of it, then," Pilgrim said. "This chalk, I been holding it so long it's starting in to melt."

"The Pells don't never give up," Trubee said. "When they start in to do something...."

"Trubee," the old man said.

"Now, there he is again," Trubee said, "You can't turn around without you find him in back of you."

"Trubee, come on down off of that stack."

"Hanging around, hanging around, all the time hanging around. He's trying to spoil my shot, that's what he is, but it ain't going to do him any good because there ain't nothing can spoil a Pell's shooting when he sets his mind to it. Pass me over that Johnnie Walker, Martin. That's what I been needing right along."

"Listen, Trubee," the old man said.

"Now, I'm asking you if that ain't a terrible thing the way he keeps on hanging around. By Christ, here I am shooting against all kinds of odds. The way he goes on talking and trying to spoil my shot, you'd think it wasn't enough to have that bottle doing a jig right on the gunsights. How can a man keep his hands steady with all that staring going on?"

"Shoot off that gun," Flood said.

"Wait'll I find the chalk," Pilgrim said. "It fell down here in the hay."

"Don't wait for nothing," Flood said. "Take your shot."

"Take a shot?" Trubee said. "Now, that's a good idea. That's just what I been thinking of. Take a shot, says Martin Flood, the wild horse from the plains of Nebraska, and what does little Trubee do? He takes a shot."

Trubee turned his head and dumped a fourfinger slug of whisky down his throat. He handed the bottle to Pilgrim.

"Here goes," he said. "This is going to be a bull's eye."

Once more old man Pell looked for the mark. A hundred feet away from the haystack a rosette of sunlight burst from the shoulder of a whisky bottle. The bottle was standing on one of the headstones in the little family graveyard at the edge of the woods.

"Trubee!" the old man cried.

The word was lost in the explosion of the repeater. The bullet missed the bottle by at least two feet, but down on the woodgray face of the headstone a round white scar appeared.

"Lousy," Pilgrim said. "You only get three out of ten for that shot."

The old man walked over to the graveyard and stood there with his hat in his hand. Leaning against the iron pipe that fenced off the plot, he looked down at the score of stones that faced him. Bottles had been set up on each of them, but only one remained. Scattered on the graves below the other stones were chunks of broken glass and torn pieces of black label. Almost every stone in the yard wore a couple of fresh white craters among the inscriptions; some of the names and dates were chipped away.

"One side, farmer!" Flood shouted from the haystack across the field, and then, before the old man had a chance to move, he pulled the trigger.

The bullet struck the top of one of the stones and bounced off into the woods. The old man listened to its highrising drone as it passed through hundreds of leaves, and then there was a distant chug, like the single stroke of a woodpecker, as the bullet buried itself in a tree.

"Still lousy," Pilgrim said. "You only get a two."

CHAPTER SIX

They stayed drunk for a week, and then one morning Trubee woke up feeling as sick as a dog. He dragged himself out of bed and puked through the window. Hanging halfway outside and pressing his belly against the windowsill as hard as he could, he made so much noise with his bubbling and gurgling that Flood woke up, too.

"What's a matter, Trubee? Up the pole too much?"

"Guess so, Martin. My gut feels like it's flapping its wings and trying to fly."

"Get back in the bunk and have another doss. I'll go see if there's any blackjack in the house."

When Trubee was in bed again, Flood went downstairs to look for a physic. He found nothing but a few moldy Cascarets, so he climbed up to the attic, where Pilgrim was lying dead to the world on a cot near the trapdoor.

"Wake up," Flood said, kicking the bottom of the cotspring. "You're going down to Warrensburg."

"I'm whacked," Pilgrim said, turning his back to Flood and starting to go to sleep all over again.

"Don't argue the toss with me, Turd. Ease up on them deskhooks and turn out or you stop one with your clock."

Blanketed to his pimply chin, Pilgrim opened his eyes. "What time is it?"

"Pretty near ten."

"Night time," Pilgrim said, and his eyes began to close.

"I give you once more," Flood said.

Pilgrim looked up at him. "Trying to make me click again, Martin?"

"Sure. Did you think I was going myself?"

"Christ, what a trip that is!"

"Take the horse and wagon."

"It's me every time. I told you yesterday you wasn't topkick around here."

"I know you did," Flood said, "only I was too stiff to do anything about it." He upended the cot, and Pilgrim rolled out on his behind. Flood reached down, grabbed the little man's arm, and yanked him to his feet. "Get moving, you pantsrabbit," he said.

Pilgrim turned away and started to get dressed. Flood went downstairs again, and when Pilgrim joined him, he handed over eight pints of the Johnnie Walker wrapped up in sheets of newspaper.

"Cash in on them, bowlegs," Flood said. "Try the pillstore first off, and if they don't want no part of you, see if you can peddle the booze in back of the hotel. Use what you get to buy the stuff I got on this list here that I made up." Flood handed over a piece of paper. "And God help you if you salvage a cole out of that money. Hitch up and get rolling."

When Pilgrim drove past the house a little later, Flood stopped him. "If you find any weasels down there, bring them back with you. I'm just about due. I'm starting in to get hot in the biscuit."

Pilgrim said, "I'll have a look." Then he headed off in the direction of the Pond and Warrensburg.

Since coming to the farm, he hadn't been off it once, and even though he'd argued with Flood about making the trip, he was really glad to be on his way. He thought Flood's idea about the broads was a good one, and he knew that he'd have looked for some even if he hadn't been told to. He was pretty near ripe for a dirtyneck, he thought. He'd had his last one in Hoboken about four weeks before, and she'd been a lousy madamoisook if there ever was one. A lousy madamoisook, a greasy waterfront push. She'd had sawdust on the back of her coat when she came out of that alley and waved goodbye to the man that came out with her. Sawdust on the back of her coat! What the Hell was dames coming to if they'd do it for you in a crate? The twobit tramp!

A cottontail rabbit bounded into the road ahead of the wagon. Propped on its forelegs, it flagged its ears before popping away between a couple of rocks and losing itself among the bushes at the edge of the forest.

Far ahead, at the bottom of a slight grade, Pilgrim saw a brown object in the middle of the road, and thinking that it was a rock, he paid no attention to it. When he got near, the object rose up out of the gravel and stood still. It was a partridge hen. Pilgrim stopped the wagon and wondered why the bird wouldn't move. From the brush at the roadside, he heard a thin whistling sound, and then the hen got stiff all over and came for the horse's legs. The chickens called again, but the hen didn't even look in the direction that the sound had come from. Instead, she stuck her head out at the horse. The horse stood where he was, so the partridge flared her wings open and beat them in the dust. Still trying to take the horse away from the hidden chickens, she made believe her wing was broken. Dragging it at her side, she made a couple of limping circles and then lit out for the side of the road opposite where the chickens were. She disappeared in the tall grass. The chickens kept quiet, and not a sound came from either side of the road.

Pilgrim stopped the wagon again in front of the lodge and went around to the well to get himself a drink. He thought of taking some water back to the horse, but forgot all about it when he began to wonder what was inside of the house. With a hunk of iron that he found near the well, he pried open one of the wooden shutters. Then he tapped the glass out with the iron and climbed into the building. The one window let in very little light, so Pilgrim fumbled around until he found the doorlatch.

After he'd opened the door, there was enough light for him to see everything in the two front rooms.

The smaller one was fixed up as a diningroom. The other had a centertable, a couch, a few rockers, a pile of folded rugs, and a bookcase filled with old newspapers and magazines. On top of the case there was a collection of fanshaped fungi, now as hard as oak, and on these people had scorched their names, the dates of their trips to the lodge, and a few lines of poetry. Pilgrim read them all. He liked the ones with rhymes:

> *Noveber, 1904*
> *Now Harry Reoux hes quite a cheff*
> *Thats what I m a shouting*
> *Till the time you all go deff*
> *That is all but his muffens*
> *On this Viele Pond venison frolic*
> *And all but his stuffings*
> *They give us all the collic.*
>
> > *Fatty Secor*
> > *A. Updegrove*
> > *Josh Backus*
> > *Thos. Greenaway*

Finding nothing that he could realize a dime on, Pilgrim opened a door of the bookcase to see if anything were hidden behind the stacked magazines. Some of them fell to the floor as the tight panel came loose. They were called "Spicy Paree," and on the front cover of each there was a photograph of a naked woman. When Pilgrim saw the pictures, he lost track of what he'd been looking for. Taking every copy of "Spicy Paree" that he could find, he locked the door of the house and got out of it the same way he'd gotten in. After wedging the shutter closed with a chip of rock, he climbed aboard the wagon again and went on toward Warrensburg.

The first magazine that he looked at ran a dozen pictures of fat French models in a section called "Our Art Gallery," which appeared after the last story in the number. The stories had titles like "The Venturesome Virgin" and "Chaste, Chased, and Chastened," but Pilgrim had no eye for stories and didn't waste his time reading as much as a line of them. All he wanted to see was the pictures, and he saw plenty.

The coozies was mighty nifty, but what the Hell was the idea of them wearing veils that hung down off of their shoulders? All them veils did was get in the way of the stuff you felt like having a look at, the good stuff. Some of the dames didn't have no veils, but they was wriggled around to one side, with the front knee bent and the front hip chucked up kind of sassy, just enough to hide the home plate. There was a whole lot to look at, nice fat hips, neat legs, juicy arms, but who wanted to wear his eyes out on some God damned arms and legs? The pictures was a plain ordinary gyp, even the ones where there wasn't no veils and where the hustlers was looking at you head on, because the guy that took the pictures had got wise and painted a sort of fog right slap over the big stuff, and you couldn't see it very good. Now what kind of an idea was that—snapping a picture of a piece with all of her clothes off, and then blocking off the good parts? It was just about the dumbest thing in the world. It was enough to make a guy so sore that he wouldn't buy the magazine no more. That picturetaker wasn't no damned good. He should of got shot instead of being paid.

Even though Pilgrim didn't like the way the pictures had been printed, the more he stared at them the more uncomfortable he became, and finally he felt so rotten that he could hardly stay on the wagonseat. His legs itched him so much that he had to drop the reins and give the horse its head while he scratched himself hard enough to heat the tips of his fingers. No matter how deep he dug them into his flesh, he couldn't reach the place that bothered him. His legs felt as if they were filled with seltzerwater. Every time he scraped them, another string of bubbles broke loose and crawled up underneath his skin.

By the time the wagon had reached the place where the road began to slope downhill, the itch was so bad that Pilgrim wondered whether he'd have to scratch himself down to the bone in order to get rid of it. It was a bitch of an itch, he thought. He'd never had anything like it. The blood in his legs was like vichy, and it tickled him as it was pumped through his veins. One minute he felt like laughing, and the next he wanted to holler his head off. It was a bitch of an itch.

Taking another look at the pictures, he climbed down off the wagon and walked alongside of the horse, holding the slack reins under its head with one hand and grating away at his legs with the other. He couldn't take his mind off the photos, especially the one where the naked woman was stretched out on a rug, propped up on her elbows; she was pointing a finger and winking at a stuffed Teddy bear on the floor in front of her. The bear looked surprised, as if the woman had sneaked up behind it and whispered something dirty in its ear.

She was a peach, that piece was, about as neat as anything he'd ever saw in his whole life, and the best part of it was that she didn't look like no ordinary bum. If he only had her in the woods right now! A broad like that!

He stopped looking at the road. He stopped thinking. His clothes were soaked with sweat. His legs were no longer solid flesh and bone; they were seidlitz powders that foamed up into the rest of his body as if they were going to blow the top of his head off. His hands slid along the reins and touched the under side of the horse's head. He walked more and more slowly all the time. He began to limp. Finally he stopped moving altogether and stared across the hills.

That broad with the Teddy bear!

His hand stroked the horse's head, slowly, always down, and soon it felt as if it didn't belong to his arm. The feel of the horsehairs made it strange, as if he'd been rubbing it back and forth over the nap of a rug. He made faster and faster strokes, deeper into the vulcanized rubber of the horse's jaws. He canted his head until the yellow polkadots of his face were buried in its cheeks. The horse cocked a hind hoof. It blinked a few times and then kept its eyes closed.

"Something the matter with the horse?"

Pilgrim came back to life. He had both arms around the horse's neck. A man was leaning over a fence and watching him.

"No, nothing," Pilgrim said. "I was just trying to calm him down."

"He takes a sight of it, then," the farmer said. "You been calming him pretty near five minutes now."

"He got ascared of a hunk of paper a little way back."

"You don't tell. Looks to me like Walter Pell's horse."

"That's right," Pilgrim said. "How do you know?"

"Sold it to him. Didn't have no use for the animal after he'd went blind."

Pilgrim looked at the man for a moment, and then said, "Well, I guess I'll be going along now." He climbed back on the wagon and slapped the reins against the horse's rump. The horse didn't start right away. Its hind legs were stretched back, and between them a thick greengold stream was pouring into the dirt.

Pilgrim had to look at the magazines again when the wagon had gone only a few hundred yards further down the road. He picked one of them up, and the first thing that caught his eye was an advertisement on the back cover:

True Blue

I have a sweetheart for you.

Under this heading, there was a sketch of a smiling boy, naked except for a box of arrows slung across his shoulder. The boy was holding one of the arrows in his hand and writing a letter with it. Pilgrim read the rest of the advertisement:

Let us arrange a hot, tingling, romantic correspondence for you. Meet your mate and sweetheart through the world's foremost correspondence club, a club for lonely and refined people who desire speedy contact with those they love, but have never met. We have the names. *We have your mate on file.* Satisfied members in each of the 48 states of the Union. Efficient and dignified service. We have made thousands of lovely people happy. *Why not you?* Send address and One Dollar (Cash, not Check), and have all your dreams come true.

True Blue Club
Mrs. Wanda Kranz
Box 412
Wichita, Kansas.

Now Harry Reoux hes quite a cheff. *Let us arrange a hot, tingling, romantic correspondence for you.* All but his muffens. *A club for lonely and refined people.* They give us all the collic. *We have made thousands of lovely people happy.* If he only had a calico out in the woods under a tree! A bottle of Johnnie Walker and a calico like the one fiddling around with the Teddy bear. Or how about nice and snug up in a hayloft, sunk way down in the stuff? Hay was a Hell of a sight better than sawdust. The Hoboken push! The twobit tramp! "Dearie," she'd called him. Why did them pots all call you "Dearie?" The damned greaseball! For another nickel, she'd of called him anything. She'd stunk out loud. Phooey, but she was punk! *True Blue, I have a sweetheart for you.*

Maybe it'd be worth his while writing to that Kranz woman out in Wichita. Flood wouldn't wise up that he'd hooked a buck out of the booze money. If he only remembered, he could fake a spiel about selling the stuff for less dough. If he got twenty, he could say nineteen—sure, if he remembered! Was it worth taking a chance about? If some broad was dumb enough to answer his letter, he might be able to sell her the idea of coming up to the farm. And then what? Nothing but one long picnic. That's what it'd be—a picnic!

The road crossed the Schroon River and joined the state highway. About a mile north of the junction, Pilgrim reached the main part of Warrensburg, a group of about half a dozen houses on each side of the pike. In the window of one of these hung three big globes of glass filled with colored water. Pilgrim stopped there, went inside, and asked for the owner.

"I'm the owner," said the man behind the counter. "Name's Bertrand. What can I do for you?"

"I got some Grade A whisky outside in my wagon. It's yours for two bucks a pint."

"Sorry," Bertrand said. "I'm not in the market." He started walking away in order to wait on another customer.

"What's the big hurry?" Pilgrim said. "How about a buck fifty?"

"I don't want your liquor. There's the door."

Pilgrim drove around to the back entrance of the Adirondack Inn. A porter came through a screendoor and began to beat a broom against a sawbuck.

"Been around here long?" Pilgrim said.

"Not so very," the porter said. "What's it *to* you?"

"That's city talk. I guess you been around."

"Some. Been to New York twothree times."

"I had it figured out you was pretty smart for a hotel porter."

"Want something?"

"Take a guess."

The porter sat down on the sawbuck and pulled a straw out of the broom. He rammed it between his teeth and spat out a white rag of food.

"Girls?" he said.

"Take a front seat."

"I got a hard time myself," the porter said. "I got to go all the way to Glens Falls for it."

"What for? With so many dames around here?"

"Not so many. The waitresses don't do me no good. They don't get much time off, and when they do, they're so fagged that all they want's an auto ride and an icecream cone. When they get to feeling good, they sell it to the guests."

"I didn't say nothing about waitresses, did I? How about farmgirls?"

The porter laughed.

"Let me in on it," Pilgrim said.

"Farmgirls?"

"I said farmgirls. What about it?"

"You been reading too many dirty stories. Get funny with the folks that live around here, and you'll get your pratt all fouled up with buckshot."

"Then what's a guy to do?"

"If I was you," the porter said, "and I didn't have no girl all to myself when I felt like it, I'd try out the Widder. She lives over to the other side of the river, near the lumberyard."

"She any good?"

"Well, she's no springchicken no more, but for a dollar you don't get no Lillian Russells nowheres."

"I'm tired of them dirtynecks. I'm still set on a farmgirl."

The porter said, "Maybe you want me to speak out for you."

"You didn't hear me say that. I mean if I could only get a hold of somebody that knows one."

"I'll ask some of the farmers when they go by," the porter said. "I'll ask them which one has a daughter he can loan you for a couple of nights. But in the meantime you better take my advice. Try out the Widder. She's a lot better than you think. Her husband got killed in the war."

"Her husband got killed over in France?" Pilgrim said. "She can't be so old, then."

"Who said France? He got killed in Cuba in the Spanish-American War, but take my word for it the Widder don't look her fiftyodd."

"Break your leg, buddy," Pilgrim said. "You ain't helping me none."

The porter laughed again and started to go back into the hotel.

"How'd you like a drink of the best Scotch in the world?" Pilgrim said.

"Bring it out."

"Come on in the barn."

Inside the barn Pilgrim opened one of the bottles and handed it to the porter. After taking a long drink, the man returned the bottle.

"What do you say?"

"God damned good," the porter said.

"It'll cost you two bucks a bottle."

"How many you got?"

"Eight."

"Give you twelve dollars for the lot."

Pilgrim started to drive out of the barn.

The porter told him to wait. He came back in a little while with a roll of bills. He counted off fifteen, claiming that he wouldn't be able to sell the open bottle.

"That's your tough luck," Pilgrim said. "Drink it yourself."

The porter gave him another bill and took the bottles.

"Any time you want it, I can get you some more," Pilgrim said.

The porter said that he could use about twenty bottles a week for the hotel trade.

After telling the man to look for him in a few days, Pilgrim drove away. He pulled up at the post office, and there he bummed an envelope and a few sheets of paper from the postmaster. He went over to the walldesk to write a letter to Mrs. Wanda Kranz:

May 22, 1920

Dear Mrs. Wanda Kranz

I seen your ad in Spicy paree about the True Blue club and I am writing you a letter so as I can join the club with one Dollar which I am inclosing here in this envelop.

I suppose you will be wanting to know what I am and do for a living as you have a good right to know seeing you will try to put me in the way of some body that will make me happy. Me being what you might call lonely and refinned like you said in your ad.

Well I am a farmer living in this state just about all my life with a good paying farm which my father left me in his will. Robert Pilgrim was his name and mine is Jas. Pilgrim as you will find out when you get at the bottom of this letter with the farm going to over 2 hundred acres all good farm land and gives crops all the time yearly so I been able to lay a little by for a rainy day.

I live on the farm all by myself with exeption of an old Aunt very nice and refinned woman God fearing. By name Rachel Pilgrim my father sister telling me all the time over and over again it is high time I should be getting maried so I will have children to give it to and help me with the working of it. Up to now I never listened to her. Minding my own bussiness and kep on working as usualy laying by good money in the bank but in the last year or so I begin thinking may be she is right my aunt Rachel and I should be getting some body to help me look after the place. The farm I mean.

I can say I got a good caracter because that is what every body knows me say and the Paster too. I am a protestent going to church regular without fail once a week all my life never missing a Sunday rain or shine. So you can see I got a good caracter and I will be good to a woman that is my True Blue wife. I say True Blue because that is the name of your club.

So Mrs. Wanda Kranz if you know any body can come up to New york state and be a farmers wife if she is a protestent I am certenly greatful for that favor. For which I am inclose one Dollar.

I am 30 years of old in very good shape never sick a day being tall and way 175 pound standing a hard days work like a real man and never tired out from it. It is not like of me to bost but my freinds which there are manny of will say I am not such a bad looking 1. And having a little money layed by in the bank they are saying may be I am a good catch for a nice refinned woman.

So Mrs. Wanda Kranz I am closing with thanks for you taking care of me this way and will promis to do the same of any body you tell them to write to me looking to marage some time in the near future. And if I am satisfed I will tell all my freinds that you had a very good club and they should hurry up and take avantage and do the same.

Inclose please find one Dollar.

Yours respectfully
Jas. Pilgrim
General Delivry Warrensburg New york.

After mailing the letter, Pilgrim went back to Bertrand's and bought a bottle of BromoSeltzer for Trubee. Then he crossed the road to the A. & P. for the rest of the articles that Flood had ordered. The list was a long one because hardly anything in the way of groceries was left at the farm. The clerk wrapped them in a large brownpaper bag, and Pilgrim took them outside and stowed them in the wagon.

He was about to drive off when he changed his mind about telling Flood that he'd gotten only fifteen dollars for the Johnnie Walker; Flood would want to know who'd bought the whisky, and it might be that some time he'd meet the porter and find out that part of the money had been drained off. It was a whole lot safer, Pilgrim decided, to jack up the prices he'd paid for the groceries; he couldn't be nailed at that if he knew what each one had to cost in order to bring the total up to cover the dollar he'd spent to join the Club and the two cents he'd laid out for a postage stamp. He went back to the A. & P. and asked for a bill.

"Where's the bag?" the clerk said.

"Out in the wagon. Why?"

"It'll be all right, I guess. No trouble to make out a bill. Now, what did them things all come to again?"

"Eight seventy."

"That's right, eight seventy," the clerk said. "Let's see how we got that figure. Be easier if we had that bag, but don't you bother to bring it in again."

After a moment or two, the clerk pushed a bill across the counter. Pilgrim put it in his pocket and left the store. On the way back to the farm, he studied the prices, raised a few, and then threw the bill away.

Flood was waiting for him under a tree in the yard. Pilgrim waved to him and drove into the barn to unharness the horse.

Flood followed him and said, "Where's the money?"

Pilgrim stuck his hand in his pocket and pulled out five bills and some loose change. He gave it all to Flood, who counted it and then looked up sideways at him.

"Shell out, Jock," Flood said, holding out his hand. "Kick in with the rest."

Pilgrim made believe he was very busy with the harness and talked to Flood over his shoulder. "That's all there is left," he said. "I sold the booze for sixteen bucks, and the stuff you had on the list come to nine seventytwo without the Bromo. How much you got there?"

"Five eightyeight, but I don't figure you spent all the rest on the groceries."

He fired off a string of questions about the price of each item, and Pilgrim answered him so quickly that Flood was sure he was lying. Without saying anything, he took the bag of food out of the wagon and looked at it. Pilgrim passed him on the his way out of the barn. As he went by, Flood stuck out his foot and kicked one of Pilgrim's in back of the other. The rear one knocked the front one up in the air, and down went Pilgrim flat on his spine. Flood put one of his boots on the side of Pilgrim's face and held it down hard against the splintery planking.

"You bowlegged bastard!" Flood said. "I got a good mind to conk you. Where's that other buck, you hotstuffer?"

"What other buck? What buck you talking about? For Christ's sake, get your hoof off of my clock."

"You know what buck I mean, you lousy sneak. On this here bag, it adds up to eight seventy. That makes a buck fortytwo you're short. How much did the Bromo cost you?"

"Forty cents."

"How about the other buck two? What did you do with it, you hardheaded crook?"

"Let me up, I tell you. You're busting my pan in."

Flood took his boot away. On Pilgrim's face, there was a small horseshoe of red pocks from the heel nails. Pilgrim got up and rubbed his cheek.

"There's some mistake, Martin," he said. "That bag must of been used for somebody else. That's all I can say. That God damned clerk must of put our stuff in a bag that he'd been figuring something else out on. I didn't have to tell you I got sixteen bucks for the booze. I could of said fifteen if I wanted to hook a buck out of it. This is what I get for being honest with you. If you think I salvaged anything out of that sixteen, you can frisk me, and be God damned to you. I'm sick of getting kicked around for nothing." He opened his coat and put up his hands. "Go on, frisk me. Look in my pockets. Look in my ears and under my arms. Look in back of my tonsils. Look up my brown. Maybe I stuck the bill in there, and the two cents, too."

Flood said, "O. K., Jock. I take your word for it, but you sure took a Hell of a time down there. What was you doing?"

Pilgrim took the magazines out from under the wagonseat and walked back to the house with Flood.

"What was I doing?" he said. "I was looking for ginch—that's what."

"Find any?"

"Nothing but the town Widder at a buck a try. I was told she wasn't so bad, but I put it off till I feel a little harder up."

CHAPTER SEVEN

Near Tuckerton, New Jersey, a narrow dirt road left the Atlantic City pike and bent east toward the ocean through the pines that cluttered the sand dunes. The road ran down to a point that sprouted like a nipple from the mainland between Great Bay and Little Egg Bay, and crossing a lattice of sandbars, it came to an end on the beach of the inlet.

Not far from the head of the point, there was an old truck farm that used to belong to a man named John Wayne, but he'd been dead for some time and the only one who lived in the little unpainted house was his daughter Anna, a girl not yet nineteen years old. She wasn't pretty, but when people took the trouble to give her more than a glance, they found out after a while that they'd forgotten all about prettiness. Her face and throat and arms were browned as dark as maplewood, browned almost to the color of her hair, which she wore long, a little below her shoulders, and tied close to the back of her neck with a piece of ribbon. Her eyes were brown, too, solid brown, like pennies, and they weren't much smaller than pennies.

She'd lived on her father's farm all her life, and although the place was halfway between New York and Philadelphia, she'd never been to either. Only twice had she taken a trip to Atlantic City, which wasn't much more than thirty miles from her home. She'd gone to grade school up near the main road until her mother died, and then she'd left and never gone back. From the time she was twelve, she'd been cooking meals for her father, washing and mending his clothes, making all of her own from the oldfashioned rags that her mother had left, and in addition doing the work around the farm that was light enough for her to handle.

Whenever her father had given her an afternoon off, she'd spent the time on the ocean beach at the far side of the shoal that formed the inlet. This beach was near the southern tip of a twentymile sandbar. Nobody lived within five miles of it, and except for a few fishermen during the summer months, hardly anybody ever went there. Anna used to put on her bathingsuit at the farm, wrap a towel and something to eat in a square of rubber cut from an old raincoat, strap the package to her waist, and then swim over to the sandbar, a distance of about a quarter of a mile at low tide.

Nobody had ever gone with her, and she'd never wanted company. She liked best of all to sit alone on the beach, facing the ocean and watching the waves curve over and smash themselves to pieces before rushing up across the sand to spread a scalloped fringe of foam at her feet. Looking at the water and listening to its steaming wash as it churned over the pebbles and shells, she'd sit on the beach for hours and hours, moving back only when the surf slid up too close to her feet. Once in a while she'd take a swim in the ocean, but most of the time she just sat on the sand and looked at the water.

She listened to its varying sounds. She remembered the many things that were brought in and stranded by the waves—shells, stones, bits of wood, bottles, brightcolored crabs, and a dozen different kinds of waterweed. Lying very still, she followed with her eyes the railbirds that blurred along the tideline, plover and snipe, thinlegged birds that ran so fast that they looked like little balls of feather being swept down the beach by the wind.

She liked to look at the sand, too. She liked to pick up a handful of it, that at first seemed to be only a dull tan, and spread the grains and hold them close to her eyes, where she could see that the dull tan was really a mixture of black and white and many brilliant colors. There were specks as black and powdery as pepperdust, and others were like glass, some transparent, some scratched and opaque. The yellow grains were pollen. The red grains were garnets, the pink coral, and the blue ones chips of frozen spray. The orange bits were lollipops, and the dark brown were sunflower seeds.

In the summer and fall afternoons, the girl never left the beach until she'd seen the iron shadows in the clouds turn to pink, and then lavender, and then purple. She liked to look away and forget the colors she'd been staring at, and then turn back after a while to see a cloud that'd been pigeongray now floating rose or salmon, like the flamingoes she'd seen in her geography book.

One day, about six months after her father's death, she'd gone over to the beach as usual. When she neared the shoal, swimming hard to make her way through the rip that was always in the channel at low water, she noticed a canvascovered dinghy heeled over on the sand. Knowing that some fisherman had come from the mainland or from the northern end of the bar, and not caring to spoil her day by running into him, Anna waded out of the water and walked south for almost a mile before crossing the belt of knifegrass to reach the ocean side of the shoal.

Coming to the low shelf curving up from the beach, she looked around her for a moment and then jumped down to the sand. She almost landed on a pile of gear belonging to the fisherman. He was sitting with his back up against the hummock she'd just been standing on. In one hand he was holding a sandwich, and in the other a bottle of beer.

"Hello you," he said.

Anna moved away without answering him.

"Want something to eat?" he called after her. "I got enough here to last me a week."

Anna didn't stop until she realized that the end of the bar was right in front of her; if she went any further, she'd be rounding the tip of it and going back up the inlet side without having spent any time on the beach. She headed the other way, and when she passed the man he spoke to her again.

"You don't have to be afraid of me, miss," he said. "I don't go around biting people."

He didn't sound like one of those rough fellows that she'd read about in stories; he didn't look as if he'd get fresh and say a lot of things that he figured were pretty smart. He had a nice voice, she thought. When she looked at him, he was smiling.

Anna smiled, too, and said, "Oh, I wasn't afraid."

"Then come on over and help me eat some of this grub."

"I got some of my own."

"Where?"

"Right here in this pack."

"You can't have an awful lot of it, then," he said. "Open up the pack and let's have a look at it."

Anna unrolled the package. She took out her towel, spread it over the sand, and then sat down on it, crosslegged, facing the ocean.

"Well, where's all that food you were talking about?" the man said.

"Right in there," Anna said, pointing to a flat little bundle about the size of a book.

"You mean to say that's all you brought with you for a day on the beach? What's in there, anyway?"

"Oh, some bread and butter, and a piece of cheese, and a hardboiled egg."

"My God!" the man said. "Take a look at this." He flipped open the cover of a wicker hamper. In addition to sandwiches, fruit, and cake, it held a masonjar loaded with pieces of cold roast chicken, and in a separate compartment several bottles of beer. The man laughed, saying, "Now, that's what I call food. Bread and butter and cheese! My God!"

The girl said, "I don't eat so very much. What I got there'll do for me."

The man twisted the cap off the jar. "Try part of this bird."

"I don't think I better."

"Why not?"

"Well, I don't like to take anything off of people I don't know."

"That's foolish," the man said. "You've been sitting here, haven't you? And you've been talking to me. If you can do that, you can eat my food."

"That's different."

"All right, then," the man said, getting up from the sand. "Let's get to know each other. My name's George English. What's yours?"

"Anna Wayne."

"Glad to know you, Miss Wayne," English said, putting out his hand.

Anna laughed as she shook hands with him. "Glad to know you, Mister English."

"Now we're friends," he said. "Change your mind about the chicken?"

"Maybe I'll try some, after all."

English talked while she ate her lunch. He said that he'd come down from Bayonne that morning to have a try for a striper or a drum, if he had the luck to hook into one. He'd knocked off only a little while before Anna came; the sun was strong, he said, and out past the breakers the water was so calm that when a sixounce sinker hit it the splash looked as if it'd been made by a bomb. All morning he'd been casting into the sheets of mullet that'd been breaking water, but he hadn't had a single strike to show for four hours of work. He didn't know what'd been making the mullet break like that, he said; it might have been one of the bass he was after, and again it might have been a big blue giving them the devil from underneath, but whatever it was he was going to peg away with every known kind of bait until he got a little attention.

He showed Anna some of his tackle and told her about split-bamboo rods, springbutts, freespool reels, how big the drum ran, the different kinds of fish he'd landed off the Jersey coast. He said that during the shark scare the year before he'd caught a seven-footer on a ganghook that'd been buried in a pound of steak. He told her about how he'd once been playing a king that he'd lured while trolling for a striper off Deal, and how a hawk had plopped into the breakers and swiped the king right out from under his nose.

Anna listened to the fisherman's talk for more than an hour. She thought he was nice because in all that time he didn't say a single thing that was out of the way. He just sat where he was, leaning back against the sandbank, smoking, waving his hands while he talked, and talking very quickly.

When he finally got up, he said that he was going to try a few more casts, and that if Anna didn't feel like going along with him, she could read one of the magazines he had in the pocket of his slicker. Then he left her and went over to where he'd sunk the butt of his rod into the sand. He stripped off the dried bait, threaded the hooks through fresh pieces of lure, and made his first cast. Followed by the tackle whirling on its swivel, the sinker shot through the air in a long low curve, and was about to clear the last line of breakers when the line fouled on the spool of the reel. The line broke, making a sound like the snapping of a twig, and the free sinker took the tackle to the bottom with it. The man got angry and was about to start swearing when he noticed that Anna was watching him. Instead of swearing, he grinned and got to work rigging on fresh tackle.

Anna looked at the magazines. One of them was called "Spicy Paree," and she was surprised when she turned its pages and found several pictures of naked women. After looking at a few of them, she closed the magazine and reached over to put it back into the fisherman's slicker. As she did so, she spotted an advertisement on the back cover. There was a drawing of a laughing boy, and under that the heading:

True Blue
I have a sweetheart for you.

Then she read through the rest of the advertisement, even the words

True Blue Club
Mrs. Wanda Kranz
B0x 412
Wichita, Kansas.

English called out to her, saying that he'd just had a hard strike. Anna got up and walked over to where he was standing. He watched her come toward him up the beach. He watched the tightening of the muscles in her thighs, the rising and falling of her hips, the sideway swing of her breasts. When she stood alongside of English, looking down the slightly sagging line to where it sliced the icing of the breakers, he asked her if she'd mind holding the rod for him while he lit his pipe. She took the rod, and he stood behind her to shield the matchflame. He looked at the white hollows of flesh under her arms. He smelled the dried salt on her body and hair. Then he dropped his pipe and grabbed the girl around her chest. The move was so sudden that he was able to shove his hands down into her bathingsuit and pinch her nipples before she could drop the fishingrod and free her own hands. He tried to bend her over backward and kiss her mouth, but she twisted her body and his teeth left brackets on her shoulder.

"Come on, baby, give us a kiss," he said. "Let's you and me have a good time."

"Take your hands off!"

"What are you being—kittenish? Why don't you get sociable?"

"Take your hands off!"

"What do you say, kid? What do you say?"

Letting her body go loose, Anna dropped to the sand and broke away. She got to her feet before English could grab her again, and ran a few yards up the beach. She stopped to fix the shoulderstraps of her suit, all the while keeping her eyes on the fisherman. He moved after her, but she turned and ran, and this time she didn't stop until he was out of sight. Crossing the dunes, she hit the shore of the inlet not far from English's dinghy. She waded out to deep water and then pushed off into the rip. She cut across this on an angle and headed for the mainland.

When she got home, she went up to her room, took off her bathingsuit, and dried herself in front of a mirror that hung over a white commode. The mirror had a birchbark border filled with tinted photographs of Niagara Falls and The Thousand Islands. With the towel behind her, Anna drew it from side to side, and looking up at the mirror, she noticed how her breasts swung a little as she worked her arms back and forth. She didn't dress herself as soon as her body was dry. She stood in front of the glass and looked at her reflection. She stood with her hands at her sides, but after a moment she raised them and touched herself where the man had touched her.

The girls at school used to say that whenever a fellow took you out he wanted to stick his hand under your dress and touch your skin; they'd said that that was called feeling you up, and that if you didn't let the fellows do it they wouldn't go out with you any more. But the girls'd been talking about fellows, about men like English. A sweetheart, though, was a whole lot different. That's what it said in stories, and stories always told you the truth. If you went out with a fellow, if you only stopped and passed the time of the day with him, you could be pretty sure that the first chance he got he was going to get fresh with you—but not a sweetheart. A sweetheart was kind. He treated you nice. He didn't ever try to stick his hand up your dress. *I have a sweetheart for you.*

She wondered why she'd never tried to get friendly with any of the young people around Tuckerton. She knew all of the boys by sight, and a lot of them to stop and talk to, but none of them had ever called on her, and none of them had ever shown any sign of wanting to. She wondered why she'd never asked anybody to go with her when she swam over to the shoal. She'd always had a good time over there all alone, but maybe she'd have had an even better one if some friend had gone along. They'd have sat on the sand together, and talked to each other about the nice things they saw in the water or on the beach or up in the sky, and when it got too warm sitting in the sun, they'd have raced off across the sand—last one in's a great big fool—and taken a dip in the ocean. If she'd gone over there with somebody, if she'd had a sweetheart, then no fellow like that fisherman would ever have gotten rough and stuck his hand inside of her bathingsuit, and nobody would have tried to kiss her unless she wanted him to. She wondered why she'd never thought of getting a sweetheart. There was so much fun at a wedding. Everybody always looked so happy and had such a good time. And then there was the honeymoon with your husband. Why, he might take you all the way to New York, or even Washington, D. C., maybe. But if she kept on the way she was going, she might never get a sweetheart to start in keeping company with her. It was nice on the beach, watching the clouds and the birds, and listening to the sound of the breakers, but it was no place to meet anybody but rough fellows like English. Maybe she wasn't so very happy after all, going around by herself all the time, not talking to anybody, not having anybody to hear about the nice things she saw, not having a sweetheart all to herself, like the girls in the stories. *Lonely and refined people. I have a sweetheart for you.*

A Pennsylvania local rocked slowly northward toward Toms River. From a window on the sunny side of one of the day-coaches, Anna looked out at a hedge of distant trees that topped the clumps of dark green grass sprouting from the sandflats.

Once in a while, through gaps in the hedge, she saw flashes of sunlight on the ocean.

Opening a straw pocketbook that lay in her lap, she took out a letter. It was postmarked Warrensburg, New York. She held the letter in her hand. She didn't read it again, for she knew every word of it by heart.

I am six foot tall and way 175 pound without my shoes and with brown hair and eyes. And my friends they say Miss that I am not such a hard one to look at. What a nice name he had! *James Pilgrim.* And he was handsome and strong, too. *I am strong and can stand my share of work like a real man being 175 and helthy like an ox never sick a day.* He'd be kind to her and not let anybody get rough like that fellow from Bayonne.

He'd feel very bad for her when she told him that she didn't like to leave her father and mother laying out there in that sandy graveyard in back of the Tuckerton church, where there weren't any flowers and trees, and where the ground was so soft that the stones were always falling down or sinking in so far that you couldn't make out the names of the people that were buried there. *James Pilgrim. James Pilgrim.* He'd see that she didn't like to think of those graves getting all untidy, and some day, without him saying a word about it beforehand, he'd have the bodies moved up to Warrensburg, and when he finally showed her the surprise there'd be a new stone with the words *Rest In Peace—John Wayne, 1858-1919, and his wife Lucille,* 1864-1913 carved on the front of it; maybe there'd even be a couple of lines of poetry, too.

Oh, he'd be good to her, all right. She was sure of it. *I can garantee a good caracter as the Paster will say of me when you see him on account of me going to church reglar without fail every Sunday rain or shine.* That's what her father had done, gone to church every Sunday even if it was snowing so hard that you couldn't see your hand in front of your face. She was sorry that she hadn't listened to him about churchgoing; she was sorry that she'd spent so much of her time laying around the beach during the summers. But just because she'd stayed away from church, that didn't make her any the less of a Protestant. It was still her religion, and she'd take it up again whenever her husband wanted her to. As soon's she got to Warrensburg, she'd learn how to pray right so's she wouldn't be making her husband *her husband, her husband* ashamed of her out there in front of the congregation.

Anna Wayne Pilgrim. The name had a good sound. If you said it very low to yourself, it was something like the ocean coming up over the sand and pebbles. *Anna Wayne Pilgrim.* In a little while, that'd be her name. It'd be her name for all the rest of her life. *Anna Wayne Pilgrim.*

She'd be very good to old Aunt Rachel. She'd wait on her hand and foot, just the same as if she was her own mother. Her own mother. She didn't know much about her mother; she been tall and thin, and as far back as she could remember, her hair had been gray; maybe it'd always been gray. But she'd make Aunt Rachel out to be her mother, and she'd live with her and take care of her all her life.

A 200 acre farm and you will have a fine room with walpaper and a nice new bed when you mary me that is soft and which I am going down to Glens Falls to by the day after tomorrow. Or which may be I will wait for you to pick out when we get back from our honymoon.

She said, "James!" She whispered it, so that nobody would hear her. "James!" she said.

Maybe Niagara Falls, like the pictures on the mirror. Maybe The Thousand Islands. What a pretty name. Were there really a thousand islands there? *When we get back from our honymoon.* He'd said something about a trip that'd last a whole week. Maybe Canada! What a trip that'd be! Only the two of them. She'd try to please him and be nice to him. Maybe he'd kiss her. Maybe he'd hold her in his arms, not rough or fresh like that fisherman fellow from Bayonne, but like a sweetheart, like a husband.

The train neared Belmar, and the conductor came down the aisle to open the door of the car. Anna stopped him and said that she'd thought the tracks ran alongside of the ocean all the way to New York. The conductor smiled and told her that if she wanted to see the ocean she'd have to change for the boatrain at West End; he said that her ticket was good on the Jersey Central, too, and that he'd let her know when to get off.

At West End, Anna had to wait half an hour for the train that connected with the Jersey Central boat. When it reached Monmouth Beach, she saw the ocean again behind a long row of mansions that backed right up to the bulkheads. After Seabright, there were no more houses on the ocean side, and between the tracks and the water there were only a narrow strip of beach and a bulkhead that was made of timber and great chunks of rough gray rock. In some places, the waves slapped up against the bulkhead and burst over the rocks, squirting spray on the windows of the car. The Atlantic Highlands highway ran along the west side of the tracks, and just beyond it was the Shrewsbury. The river was very calm, and the color of it was bottlegreen except where the long fingers of the sandbars showed through the shallows. Opposite the Sandy Hook junction, the Highlands grew straight up out of the river for three hundred feet.

When the train got a little way past Water Witch, it ran out over a long wooden trestle that ended in a dock. The "Monmouth," a white steamer with two slanting black funnels, was waiting at the dock for passengers from the train. The sail was smooth as far up as the tip of the Hook, but in the open lower bay a strong wind from the ocean made the steamer heel over and roll slowly from side to side. Beyond the Narrows, in the upper bay, Anna saw many kinds of boats that she'd never seen before—long fat ferries, barges, tugs, fireboats, freightcar scows, rusting tramp steamers riding high at anchor and flying flags that the girl didn't recognize. Near Governors Island, they passed the "Mauretania" coming down the bay, and Anna was pleased by the strings of colored pennants that were flying from the masts.

CHAPTER EIGHT

L ate in the afternoon, Pilgrim drove the Pell wagon down the main street of Lake George, past the ball field and the Court House, and then, making the bend at the foot of the lake, he pulled up opposite the sloping lawn of the Fort William Henry. He was meeting the Albany local, and he had ten minutes to spare. He looked out across the water and watched the sidewheeler "Sagamore" skid in toward the pier of the Lake Navigation Company. Behind the fresh white hull of the steamer, the woods on the far shore were as bluegreen as the lake itself.

What would she look like?

What would she look like?

Maybe she'd be a fat slob with a flat turnedup snout like a hog. Maybe she'd be a dumpy little dame with legs like hams and a puss like a melon. Maybe she'd be one of them skinny squabs that felt like you was holding an icebag. Maybe some long drink of a hick that had pointy breasts about the size and shape of a thorn. But what the Hell was the difference, anyway? If he was getting a rooking with his prize package, then the score was all even. Make believe the dame wasn't due for a falldown as soon as she clapped eyes on what was waiting for her! *Six feet tall and way 175 pound!* What a laugh! Wait till she got a flash of his five foot three and his hundred and fifteen pounds; wait till she took a squint at the guy that wasn't never sick an hour in his life, the guy that could knock off after a hard day's work without even breathing hard; wait till she looked over his two hundred acres, all good farm land; wait till she found out about his character. Why, she'd have a stroke!

And suppose she did. She'd be too far from home to let out a bleat. Home! She didn't have any now that she'd sold it to pay off her old man's debts. Let her squawk her head off. It wouldn't do her a damned bit of good. All she'd get out of her hollering would be a sore throat and maybe a smack on the side of the jaw if she got too noisy. To Hell with any dame that was going to turn out to be a louse! This one was coming upstate on her own hook, and she'd have to take potluck. She'd have to like it or lump it. But what if she looked like the end of a caboose? Suppose she was so punk that he had to turn his head away from her, even in the dark. Suppose she... but what the devil did he care? All he was after was a piece, and as long as he got that, she could look like a gorilla.

He felt the itch starting again far down in his legs. It shot up fast this time and bothered his face as if it were covered with ants. He raised his hand to scratch himself, but he stopped when he remembered the new batch of pimples that were just beginning to show through his skin. His teeth were worse than ever now, and the whiff of food turning sour in their cavities made even Flood and Trubee take good care not to get too close to his mouth. Since coming from New York, he'd lost another of his ragged greenblack splinters, and those that were left stuck out of his raw gums like slivers of dirty rock.

Six feet tall and way 175!

Never sick a day!

Hearing the whistle of the train as it started down the grade, Pilgrim drove ahead to the station. He tied the reins around one of the poles of the colonnade and went over to a baggage truck halfway up the platform; he stayed there until the train came in and the passengers got off. Most of them had gone away before he spotted the girl coming toward him from the last car.

She had her best clothes on, a suit of blue serge so faded in places that it looked gray, as if somebody had slapped it with a dusty hand; it was shiny in back, on the cuffs, and all along the seams. The skirt was too short, and the jacket was tight in the armpits and bulging at the shoulders. She wore an eggcolored straw hat that sat high up off her face and so exactly straight that it looked like a little bundle that she was balancing. Sewed onto one side of the hat was a bunch of wirestemmed paper flowers and imitation fruit, cherries and peaches and a little green apple. Some of the wires had come loose, and one of the flowers and a cherry were flopping out of the bunch and hanging down alongside of the girl's ear. She wore black cotton stockings and a pair of scuffed gray shoes. In one hand she carried a straw suitcase trimmed with brown cardboard that was grained to look like alligator leather. With the other hand she held a rolled umbrella of red cotton, a pocketbook, a bundle wrapped in brown paper, a timetable, and the latest issue of "Spicy Paree."

And what a piece!

Pilgrim slid off the truck and walked over to the girl. He took his hat off as he spoke to her.

"Hello, miss," he said.

She tried to walk around him, but he blocked the way.

"What's your hurry?" he said. "Don't you know me?"

"No, I don't. Let me by."

"I'm James Pilgrim."

The girl moved back a little and looked at him. Then she smiled, but stopped very quickly.

"I'm James Pilgrim," he said again.

This time the girl didn't smile at all. She stared at Pilgrim for a moment and then put all of her things on the baggage truck. She opened her pocketbook and looked for Pilgrim's letter.

As soon as he saw the envelope, he knew what she had in her mind. Sooner or later there'd have to be a showdown, but he'd be damned if the platform of the depot wasn't the worst place in the world for it. Once he got her away from the station and on the road to the farm, she could holler her bloody lungs out. Nobody would hear her except the skunks and the weasels out in the woods, and it'd take more than a skunk or a weasel to do her any good. He wouldn't let her off the wagon even if she wanted to walk all the way back to Lake George. Let her off the wagon! Why, if she kicked up too much of a fuss, he'd slap her one in the mouth and haul her into the bushes right then and there.

"I was only joshing you, miss," he said. "I'm not Pilgrim at all. I'm just his friend that he sent me down here to get you. Pilgrim, now, he's busy up to the farm getting it ready for you to come in. He's got a Holy Joe up there waiting to hitch you both up, and all the neighbors is out in the yard looking for the wagon already."

"It's a good thing you owned up who you was," Anna said. "I was just going to get out a letter Mister Pilgrim wrote me where he said what he looked like. Six foot tall, he is, and weighs a hundred and seventyfive. So you can see I knew all along that you wasn't him."

Pilgrim laughed, showing his stained crockery. "Don't you be worrying your head about Pilgrim," he said. "He's a mighty fine man, and that's what everybody in this country will tell you. When you get yourself hitched up to him, you'll sure be doing something that all the girls around here will be turning yellow in the face about. I might even go as far as saying that you're pretty lucky, what with Pilgrim's good money in the bank and his character and all that paying farm land. But we better be moving along, miss. It's getting late, and they're waiting on us right now."

He took Anna's things and led the way to the wagon.

The niftiest piece he'd laid eyes on in years! You ran across a dame like that about once in a blue moon, and when you did there wasn't nothing else you'd even spit on till you got yourself so blind drunk that you couldn't tell the difference between a woman and a broken bottle. By God, he was one lucky guy. The Johnnie Walker. The hayloft. The soft meat under the broad's arms and around her back. The way her hair came down and brushed her shoulders. She looked lousy in clothes, but wait till he yanked them off of her, wait till she was laying out in front of him with nothing on, wait till he got his hands on her. He was one lucky guy.

On the way up to Viele Pond, Pilgrim looked sideways at Anna every chance he got, and the more he looked the more he wished that his eyes could bore holes through her suit. The first part of the trip was no better than torture. Nothing was right, nothing was comfortable, nothing was soft or smooth. He felt as if the collar of his shirt were strangling him to death. The crotch of his pants was bunched and tight, and it was beginning to saw him in half. The springs under the wooden seat were broken, and every time the wagon hit a hole in the road and Pilgrim bounced on the splinters of the plank, he felt like cutting loose with a blast of curses that'd blow everything skyhigh; but finally, during the last part of the ride, he got the cokey feeling that he was floating in the air like a cloud. Not knowing what the girl would look like, he'd let his imagination run wild, and the result was a dream of a dame pieced together like a trick photograph. She was built up from parts of the best women he'd ever known, and looked something like the rubber figure in the advertisement for Michelin tires. She was a round and enormous nightmare, and she wallowed alongside of him like an observation balloon.

Anna looked at the countryside and paid no attention to the little man sitting on the seat with her. When the wagon reached the shoulder of Harrington Hill, she made him stop to let her take a long look at the many colors of the distant ridges in the late afternoon sunlight. She noticed all the different kinds of trees and bushes. She looked into the marshes and among the shaded clumps of fern. She looked at the clouds, the brooks, the uneven and rocky ground. Once she caught sight of a hawk, smaller than those that sailed over the inlets down in Jersey, but much faster and more brightly colored. She saw rabbits and chipmunks. She heard the music of birds that she couldn't see, and the sucking chatter of red squirrels perched high up in the beeches that lined the road.

When they passed the lodge at Viele Pond, Pilgrim thought of stopping there and taking the girl inside, but he changed his mind when he remembered the stack of whisky cases that were waiting for him at home. A long swig of the Johnnie Walker would give him just the kind of toning up that he'd need for the work he had to do. Whisky and women always went together, and one was no damned good without the other. After a good stiff shot of Scotch, he'd be a new man. He'd mosey up to the dame and kiss her right smack on the mouth. He'd kiss her all over her face. He'd take her clothes off, and then he'd kiss her all over her body, all over it, everywhere.

He could hardly wait to get started. He felt as if the farm were a hundred miles away and they were crawling there on their hands and knees. He felt as if it'd take him a month to get there. The horse was easing along so slowly that Pilgrim wanted to grab the whip and beat its God damned hide off, but he held his temper because he was afraid the girl wouldn't like to see him slamming away at the old nag; he sat still and let the dog take its own good time. They'd never get there, he thought. They'd never get there. If he only had some of that whisky now!

When the wagon turned into the Pell farmyard, Anna saw a man sitting on a treestump across the clearing. Flood took a look at the girl, and then he got up and stared.

Six feet tall and way 175!

That was James, Anna thought. He'd told the truth. He wasn't such a badlooking one. He was big and strong, and a hard day's work would only be play for him, just like he'd said in his letters. She liked his wide shoulders and the way he combed his black hair. She liked the way he held his head. She liked the look on his face. He'd be good to her.

Flood went over to the wagon and helped the girl climb down. Then he looked up at Pilgrim, who was smiling. The remains of his chin were pressed back against his throat, and he held his head like a cock getting set to crow. He winked at Flood.

"Well, what do you say, Martin?" he said. "Maybe I didn't do so bad by myself."

Martin? Anna looked from one man to the other. "Where's Mister James Pilgrim?" she said. "Which one of you is Mister James Pilgrim?"

Pilgrim said, "Tell her who Pilgrim is, Martin. Break the good news."

Flood squinted up at the little man. Then, without looking at the girl, he jabbed his thumb at his navel and said, "I'm Pilgrim, miss. I been expecting you."

Pilgrim got so excited that he nearly fell off the wagonseat. He let out a loud holler and jumped to the ground. "You lousy lying sonofabitch!" he shouted. "You know God damned well your name ain't Pilgrim."

Flood pushed the girl to one side and then turned to the little man. "You sure you ain't going crazy?" he said. "Why, you know right well I'm James Pilgrim. What's the idea of trying to make this lady think you're me?"

Pilgrim's face got very pale, the ropes of vein in his neck standing out green, like the guts of a plucked bird. He couldn't talk. Without thinking, he let fly and socked Flood as hard as he could. His fists bounced off Flood's chest like rubber balls off a brick wall, but he went right back and tried again. For Anna's benefit, Flood took a few more punches without batting an eye, and then he let Pilgrim have it. He hit him just once, flush on the side of the jaw, and Pilgrim went over as if he'd been mowed down, as if his legs had been cut off at the knees. He lay flat on his back in the dirt. His mouth filled with blood, and it ran out over his face and dripped to the ground.

Flood took the girl's things out of the wagon and told her to follow him. He led the way into the house and upstairs to the big front room. Gathering Trubee's clothes, he took them up to the attic. Then he cleaned out a few drawers in the bureau and lined them with newspaper.

Anna stood near the window and watched him. She was still wearing her hat, and the dangling flower and cherry were still rubbing the side of her face. Holding her pocketbook against her chest with both hands, she looked as if she were hugging herself. Her legs were close together and her shoulders were drawn in, as if she were trying to squeeze her body through a narrow opening. She said nothing, but watched Flood with wideopen eyes.

What a strong man he was! And how kind he looked! He'd be good to her. Anybody could see that.

When Flood finished cleaning the bureau, he went over to Anna and put his arms around her. Bending his head, he pushed a hard wet kiss deep into her mouth. She kept her arms where they were, between herself and Flood. He tightened his arms and began to move them slowly up and down the girl's back, up and down and across, up and down and across. Then he drew his hands under her arms and let them stay there for a while pressing up into the soft hollows. Then he slid them around to the sides of her breasts. He felt them through the jacket of her suit, high and round and firm. Under his halfclosed lids, his eyes rolled up until they looked like slices of hardboiled egg. Tipping her head back a little, Anna watched his face while he put his hand inside of her jacket and felt her body through the thin material of her shirtwaist. He packed her flesh with his cupped hand as if he were making a snowball, and when he reached the little buttons that he'd been making believe he couldn't find, he put his head down again and kissed the girl all over her face and on her throat and chest.

He reached up and took her hat off. Without looking, he threw it away from him. It fell on the bed, where it lay with its fruit and flowers shaking for a few seconds. He took off the girl's jacket and threw that away, too. Then he put his hands on her shoulders and tried to slip her shirtwaist down her arms. When he did that, Anna moved away from him, still keeping her hands woven across her chest.

Flood was so excited that he could hardly talk. His throat felt as if it'd suddenly been stoppered by a thick membrane. When the words came through, they seemed to pop, like airbubbles bursting from a swamp.

"What you ascared of, sister?" he said. "I wouldn't hurt you for nothing in the world. Why, you and me is going to get along fine." He moved toward her.

Anna's voice was high and thin, and it had only one tone, like the creaking of a cricket's wings.

"Who are you?" she said.

"James Pilgrim."

"That's a lie."

"Give us another kiss."

"Who are you?" the girl repeated. "What's your name? Where's Mister Pilgrim, and where's the minister?" Her hands came down and fumbled around each other over the pocketbook, as if she couldn't make up her mind how to hold it.

"You want to know where Mister Pilgrim is?" Flood said. "You want to know where the great big farmer is that sent away for you? Well, he's laying out there in the yard with a brandnew lump on his dome—that's where he is. He's the one wrote for you to come, all right, but I'm the one takes you. You're too damned good for that lousy little sneak. Why, you're one of the best pieces I ever seen in my whole life, and I'm crazy about you already. Give us another kiss."

The girl ran out of the room. When she got downstairs, Trubee was standing in the doorway. She tried to go around him, but he blocked her off by putting his hands on the jamb.

He said, "What's the rush, baby? Where you traveling to so fast?"

Over his shoulder, Anna saw Pilgrim sitting up in the yard. His hands braced his body, but his scattered legs flopped so loosely in front of him that he looked like a dummy that'd been flung up against a wall. His head sagged toward his chest, as if it'd gotten too heavy to hold up, but when he heard Trubee talking, he lifted it slowly and blinked at the doorway.

"I want to go 'way from here quick," the girl said. "I got fooled. There's no James Pilgrim a farmer around here, unless you mean that thing over there in the dirt. I come up here to get married, but I guess I changed my mind. I want to go 'way from here right this minute."

Flood came down the stairs behind her and stuck his hands under her arms. When they were around to her breasts, he pulled the girl back against him.

"There's no use of you taking on so," he said. "You're up here, and you stay here. You come out of your own free will, and even if you don't like it here now, you'll get so after a while that you couldn't tear yourself away. I'm the only one's going to lay a finger on you, and I guess I ain't so hard to take."

Trubee said, "What's it all about, Martin? Who is she, and how come she's up here?"

"The Turd, there, he joined up with a letterwriting outfit when I sent him down to Warrensburg the morning you was sick. He salvages a buck that trip, and he won't own up to it even when I knock him flat, so I know then and there that he's got something up his sleeve. I keep an eye peeled, and I find out that he rooks us on the change every time we send him out. I don't say nothing—it wasn't much, anyway—because I want to find out what he's up to. Sure enough, he gets in with a mailorder club that soaks you a buck to put you next to some lay. The only catch is that the broad might live a couple of states away, and if you want her you got to see a Holy Joe about it first. The Turd has a tough time getting started. First he hooks up with somebody in Aberdeen, South Dakota, and then he gets the name of a coozie out in Oklahoma. He writes back to the club that he wants his partner to be closer, because how the Hell can he be paying carfare for a couple of thousand miles? Well, finally he gets the tip on Miss Wayne, here. She comes from around Barnegat Bay, New Jersey, and she's here to get married to a James Turd Pilgrim, a farmer that's got a two hundred acre property." Still holding the girl's body close to him, Flood blew a laugh over her head. "How do I know all about this? First, because I'm smart, and second, because the Turd's dumb. He keeps everything under his mattress, the letters he got from the club, the letters he got from Miss Wayne, and—what do you think?—copies of the letters that he sent. I tell you, Trubee, you're going to die laughing when you read them mash notes. They was so good that I didn't do nothing about the Turd crooking our money to get in with the club and to pay for all the different names he was making them send. I don't say nothing, but I just sit back and wait to see the kind of hooker that falls for him. When this nice juicy piece comes along, though, I make up my mind it's me that gets her, not the Turd. This little broad's too swell for a brokendown jockey.... Well, that's all there is to the story."

"Suppose she don't want you, Martin?" Trubee said.

"Suppose *who* don't want me?"

"Miss Wayne."

Pilgrim was on his feet again. The lower half of his face was smeared with a paste of dust and drying blood. His shirt and hands were soaked with it. He wiped his chin with a sleeve of his coat, and then he started for the doorway. He stopped at the foot of the steps and looked at Flood's hands on the girl's chest. Trubee stood aside and watched him.

"You dirty bastard!" Pilgrim said. He wasn't shouting now; he was talking in a tone that couldn't have been heard ten feet from the doorway. His voice bubbled through his cracked lips and whipped the foam of blood and spit that'd collected in his mouth. "You dirty bastard! I didn't bring that dame up here for you to play around with. If you put a hand on her, I'll kill you."

Flood said, "I got other things to do tonight besides polishing you off like you're crying for. I got other things that's more important. But about me putting my hands on this dame—where in Hell do you think I got them now? Just in case you can't see, how about this?" He clamped his palms more tightly against the girl's breasts, and then he pressed them upward, making them swell toward the top of her shirtwaist. "And how about this, Turd?" Flood bent down and kissed the back of the girl's neck. "How about it? Do you like it, or don't you?" The girl tried to break away, but Flood held her fast and laughed out loud. "So do me something, Farmer Pilgrim. I'm waiting on you."

Pilgrim reached down and grabbed a rock off the ground, but Trubee, jumping from the top step and getting behind the little man, caught hold of his arms and pinned them back.

"Don't be a fool," Trubee said. "Maybe you want to hit the girl with that rock. Drop it, now. Don't be a fool, I tell you."

Pilgrim's voice went up high again and wavered like a child's. "I'll drop it through his stone conk, the robber. I'll bash it through his pan. I'll bust his skull wide open with it. Let me go, Trubee, and I'll kill him. I been standing his roughguy stuff a long time now, and I'm sick of it. First he kicks me. Then he knocks me down and stands on my God damned moosh. Stands on my face, Trubee! And finally he clips me with a roundhouse, and now look at me. Look at my face! Look what he done to me! Let go of my arms, will you? And all the time the sonofabitch wasn't rapping me all over the place, he was talking big, trying to throw a scare into me. By Jesus, if he don't take his hands off of that dame, I'm going to slam him over the nut with this rock. The strongarm guy! For Christ's sake, Trubee, let me go, *please!*"

Flood came down the stoop and walked over to Pilgrim. Trubee held on to the little man's arms because he thought that Flood was only going to take the rock away from him. Instead of doing that, Flood pulled back his fist and slugged him right on the point of his jaw. Pilgrim was hit so hard that his head snapped back and bounced off Trubee's cheekbone, almost knocking him stiff, too. The little man was stonecold the second the punch landed, and he dropped as if he'd been hit over the head with an axe. When he was down, Flood kicked him in the ribs hard enough to turn his body over. He stepped in to plant another one, but Trubee stopped him.

"Do you want to kill him, Martin? I'm through with you if you touch him again. I'm through with you, do you hear me?"

Flood looked at him for several seconds.

Trubee crossed over Pilgrim and stood between him and Flood. "Right now, let's go and eat," he said. "The old man's got supper ready. Come on, Martin, and you, too, Miss Wayne. Let's go inside."

Flood held back for a moment, and then he said, "All right, Trubee."

CHAPTER NINE

It was almost dark outside by the time Trubee, Flood, and Anna entered the kitchen. The table was set, and the old man had a couple of kerosene lamps going. When he saw the girl, he left the stove and walked over to Trubee.

"Who's that, Trubee?" he said, pointing a finger at the girl, but looking at his son.

"A friend of Pilgrim's."

"A friend of mine, you mean," Flood said. "What makes you ask, farmer?"

"I'm not talking to you."

"But I'm talking to *you*."

The old man spoke to Trubee again. "I want to know who that woman is."

"A friend of Pilgrim's."

"God damn it!" Flood said. "I just told you she was a friend of *mine*. And what's the idea of all the questions? Just serve up the food, farmer, and keep your puss shut, if you know what's good for you."

"This is my house," Pell said, "and I'm not standing for you bringing women up here."

"*You* won't stand!" Flood said. "Who in Hell are you to tell me what to do? I'm giving the orders around this dump."

"You're not giving *me* any. I say there's going to be no carrying on with a woman in my house. I say she's got to get out."

Flood went around the table and grabbed a handful of clothes on Pell's chest, lifting the bunch until his fist was grazing the old man's chin. "Listen, farmer," he said, "Pilgrim's laying out in the yard for saying a whole lot less. If you want to get throwed out of here on your ass, just keep on talking back at me."

Trubee said, "I don't see any sense in disputing here and now. It stands to reason we can't put a woman out in the middle of the night. Let's talk it over in the morning."

The old man looked at him for a moment and then turned again to the stove.

Flood said, "First he asks everybody to tell him who the floozie is, and the next thing you know he's busy frying up a hunk of steak. Say hello to my girl friend, old timer. Her name's kind of pretty—Anna Wayne—and she come all the way from Jersey just to see us and have a good time. This farmer here, he's Trubee's old man, Walter Pell."

"Glad to know you, sir," the girl said.

Pell answered without turning. "Please to meet you."

Trubee, Flood, and the girl sat down at the table, and the old man began to wait on them. When Anna saw that nobody was going to help him, she got up out of her chair, but Flood held her arm and pulled her down again.

"You don't have to wrassle pots, baby," he said. "That's what the old man's here for. You just take it easy and don't fag yourself out."

The girl looked at Trubee, but his head was turned the other way. The old man put a couple of platters of food on the table, and Flood helped the girl to a brimming load of it. After dumping out a plateful for himself and shooting the platter up the table to Trubee and his father, he got to work and ate steadily for ten minutes. At the end of that time his plate was empty, and he called for the platter again.

"How do you like it, baby?" he said, while his second round of food was coming down the table. "It's deer meat. Trubee and me, we shot it ourself a few weeks ago. It's getting high now, so it ought to taste pretty good. Don't be telling nobody about it, though, or the both of us, Trubee and me, we might be cooling our pants in the county jug."

Flood ate a big supper and felt very good after he'd washed it down with a couple of cups of coffee. Then, moving his chair around to the girl's side of the table, he reached over, slammed Trubee on the shoulder, and asked him for a butt.

"You got a pack right in your pocket," Trubee said.

"I left it upstairs."

"No, you didn't. Look in your pocket, the one on the right side."

Flood felt for the cigarettes where he'd been told to, and he looked surprised when he found them. "How'd you know they was there, Trubee?"

"They're always there."

"Sometimes I forget them."

"They're always there."

"Give us a light."

"You got matches, too."

"What's eating you?" Flood said.

"Nothing, except you get me sick and tired the way you expect everybody to wait on you hand and foot. You always got butts, and you always got matches, but you don't ever lift a finger to help yourself. What do you think this is, anyway? It's a wonder you don't ask us to feed you, too."

Flood looked at him and then laughed. "I guess you better take a pill, son. You sound like you got a sour stomach."

"*You* don't, though, Martin. You act like you're feeling mighty spry."

"Why shouldn't I be?" Flood said. "It was a good supper, and it feels like good sleeping weather. When we first come up here, it didn't look to me like there was going to be much fun hanging around a place that was caving in like this one is, but lately I been thinking maybe it ain't such a bad dump after all. Tell the truth, I'm looking ahead to enjoy myself."

While Flood spoke, his hand came up across the back of the girl's chair and began to play with the loose sprays of hair that fell over the collar of her shirtwaist. Trubee watched her face as she stared at the moths springing at the hot chimneys of the lamps. From where he was sitting, her cheeks looked as glossy as glass, and all the stray hair meshed around them was brightened by the flames until it shone like shavings of metal. He thought that he'd never seen anyone so pretty.

The moths shot back and forth across the table. Some of them lit on the chimneys, but after a few seconds they dropped dead on the oilcloth, curled and scorched. Others sailed right over the rims of the lamps and fell into the little hands of fire waving from the wicks. When anybody moved at the table, behind him a giant of a shadow stretched on the wall.

Trubee said, "What made you change your mind, Martin?"

"Hard to say. Sometimes you start in by not liking a thing, and then for no reason at all you find yourself switching around and thinking just the other way. The first time we come up the road here, with all them mountains and trees and rocks, I said to myself there's mighty little of a good time going to come out of all that crap. That's the way I looked at it till just lately. Till today, in fact, Trubee. Human nature, I guess."

Trubee stood up. His shadow swelled to the size of a tree, covering an entire wall.

"Maybe it's the woods, Martin," he said. "I know them better than you, and I can tell you I've saw men do plenty of funny things in the woods that they wouldn't even think of doing any place else. It's the quiet. You get a chance to think. Maybe that's what does it. If a man thinks long enough, and it's quiet and he don't get bothered any, he's apt to get kind of loony. That's where the funny things come in."

"That's a mighty long speech for you, Trubee," Flood said. "If you're meaning anything special by it, I'd like to know."

"I guess I was just talking," Trubee said, staring at the table and at the collars that the dead insects had formed on the oilcloth around the lamps. "Maybe I'm going loony myself. I better go outside and see how the bowlegged farmer's getting on."

He left the kitchen and went out into the dark.

Pilgrim was lying exactly where he'd fallen. Trubee kneeled down and helped him sit up. The little man's head slumped forward, and the blood began to drip out of his mouth again. Trubee struck a match and saw that Flood's last punch had plowed a gash down Pilgrim's face. This was drying now, and it was filled with a dusty jelly of hardening blood. Trubee took Pilgrim by the armpits and hoisted him to his feet, but there was no strength in them and the knees wobbled as if they were going to let the legs fold over backward. Trubee helped him through the yard to the pump near the barn, with Pilgrim's legs lashing out from side to side all the while as if he were dead drunk.

Trubee sat him down on the baseboards of the pump and went into the kitchen to get some towels. The old man had finished cleaning up the place, and only Flood and Anna were there. They were still at the table. Flood had moved closer to her and was doing all the talking. He didn't look up when Trubee came into the room. Trubee said nothing, but took some towels out of a cupboard and one of the lamps from the table, and then he went back to Pilgrim. He found him leaning over with his head against the neck of the pump.

"What's going on in there, Trubee?" Pilgrim said.

"Nothing much."

"What are they doing?"

"Flood's talking."

"What about?"

"I don't know. I didn't listen."

"Where are they?"

"In the kitchen."

"Still in the kitchen?"

"Yes."

"Jesus, but my puss hurts."

Trubee pumped up a bucket of water and made Pilgrim soak his head in it. Then he took a wet towel and wiped the dirt out of the cuts. When they were clean, he wet a fresh towel in the ice-cold water and held it up against Pilgrim's face until the rag got warm again. He did this several times, and finally Pilgrim said that he felt better. He stood up and thanked Trubee for helping him, and then he went off toward the barn, saying that he was going to walk around in the fields for a little while.

Trubee watched him go through the tunnel of the barn and down the back runway to the pasture. Then the little man disappeared in the dark. Trubee heard his shoes scraping along a gravel path, but the sound got smaller and smaller, and then it went away. It was very quiet in the yard.

Trubee blew out the lamp and turned to watch the light in the kitchen window. In a few moments all the shadows began to swing; the light dimmed away as somebody picked up the lamp and walked out of the room with it. As soon as the kitchen was dark, Trubee went around to the front of the house and looked up at the windows on the second floor. He watched until the swinging and brightening light became steady. Then he let himself very quietly into the house. He took his .22 out of the closet, slid some cartridges down the magazine under the barrel, and made his way upstairs so slowly and carefully that none of the boards made a sound under his feet.

Opposite the door to the front room there was a deep alcove, and at the back of this was the flight of steps leading to the attic. The alcove was almost pitchdark; the only light that Trubee could see from the steps was a sliver of it in a cracked panel of the door. Standing back in the corner, he heard Flood's voice. He heard him coaxing the girl to go to bed with him. He heard him flattering her about her mouth, her eyes, her hair, her shape. He heard him make promises. Trubee's hands shook so much that he was afraid to keep his fingers near the hammer of the rifle. They shook as if they were in a barber's vibrator, and more than once Trubee nearly dropped the gun to the floor. He heard Flood getting angry and excited. He heard him threatening the girl. At the first sound of her voice, Trubee started for the door.

He'd hardly taken a step when he heard a scratching on the floor in front of him. He stopped in his tracks. The girl's voice sounded again. She was crying. She was begging Flood to let her go. The scratching started again, this time not five feet away from where Trubee was standing. Then something got up in front of him, and he knew that it was right up against the closed door.

The girl screamed, but before Trubee could make a move, the door was opened and shoved in from the outside. Pilgrim stood in the doorway with the 30.30 in his hands.

Flood had the girl down on the bed. Most of her clothes were off, but she was holding on to the rest and trying to cover herself. Flood was sitting next to her on the bed. His shoes and shirt were off, and he was leaning over the girl, holding her down with one hand and feeling her up with the other. When he heard the door open, he spun his head around.

"Get to Hell out of here!" he said.

"Take your hands off of my girl," Pilgrim said.

"Get to Hell out of here, or I'll break your lousy neck!"

"Take your hands off of my girl."

Flood got up from the bed and limped toward Pilgrim, bending over a little. "If I touch you once more, it's going to be to conk you for fair."

"First you have to get by the hollow end of this pipe," Pilgrim said. "If you think you can do that, you bastard of a baboon, then start coming."

"You yellow little louse! For the last time, I'm telling you to blow."

"Not yellow, toughguy, just little, but this nice shiny piece of iron makes us all even. You gave me your last order, big boy, and now it's my turn. Either you come out of here and leave my girl alone or I bury a slug in that stinking dogmeat of yours. Which do you take?"

Flood dove for him.

Pilgrim snapped the rifle up and fired. The bullet stopped Flood as if he'd walked into a locomotive. As he sagged, Pilgrim tilted the barrel of the gun and deliberately shot him in the groin. The second bullet blew the middle out of Flood, and he folded up like a campchair, his head bouncing on the floorboards when he fell. Pilgrim went toward him and looked down to see if he were still breathing. Then he raised the gun again, but Trubee rushed out of the alcove and knocked up the muzzle.

He took the rifle away from Pilgrim, and put the girl out of the room just as old man Pell came to the door. Pell looked at Flood's body and then at the rifles in Trubee's hands.

"You didn't do it, Trubee!" he said. "You didn't do it!"

"No, but, by Christ, I was going to. You take care of Miss Wayne, pop. I'll see how far gone Flood is."

He closed the door and asked Pilgrim to help him lay Flood out on the bed.

Pilgrim burst out laughing. "You're asking *me*!" he said. "Why, you ought to know better than that. I don't touch meat during Lent, and I don't touch dogmeat *any* time of the year. I wouldn't lay a finger on that devil if I knew he was croaking. I hope I conked him." He sat down on a chair and lit a cigarette.

Trubee went to work and pulled Flood's pants down over his socks. High up on the left thigh a bright smear spread its crooked spokes. On Flood's shoulder there was another. Trubee cut the underwear off the body and then dragged it up on the bed.

"That shot in the middle was a beaut," Pilgrim said, leaning over and looking at it. "There's so God damned much blood around it that I can't tell if it hit him where I was aiming—right in the business. I hope I conked him for real. I hope I fixed him so's the girlies won't have no more use for him. I don't give a God damn what they do to me for it; the look on his mug when I yanked the trigger was worth anything. Surprised, the tough-guy was. Didn't think I had guts enough to plug him. Said I was yellow. *Me* yellow! Can you imagine that? He's had it coming to him a long time now, giving me the roughhouse whenever he felt like it, knocking me down, standing on my puss, laying all over my girl that way. I hope I knocked him all out of gear. I hope he's dead."

Trubee used a pillowcase to mop the blood off Flood's body. In front of his shoulder the first bullet had left an opening as clean as a nail hole, but in back it came out through a pit that looked as if it'd been made by blasting. The other shot had torn a chunk out of the inside of the thigh, not two inches from the scrotum.

"How's that one down under, Trubee? Did it get him in the business? Did I fix him so's he can't get no more fun out of his Saturday nights?"

"Shut up," Trubee said. "If I don't get a doctor fast, this punk's going to pass out cold on us. You must of busted a vein in his leg."

"How tough! My nose bleeds for him."

Trubee got a short length of twine, tied the ends, and slipped it up over Flood's leg all the way to the crotch. Then, holding a small stout bottle just above the wound, he stuck the handle of a hairbrush under the rope and twisted it until the bottle was almost buried in Flood's thigh.

"That's the best I can do for him. It'll be all over if I don't get somebody to stop the blood. I'm going to take the wagon and go down and use Bennett's telephone. In the meantime, you lay off."

"I'm disappointed about not getting him in the works," Pilgrim said. "I'm terrible disappointed."

❖ ❖ ❖

Remembering every bump and turn in the road, Trubee beat the horse into a gallop and kept him at it through the darkness until they reached the upgrade that ended at the lodge. There he put the whip away and gave the horse a breather, and they were nearing the crest of the rise when Trubee spotted a figure running over the weaving pattern of light and leaves that lay on the road before him. He touched up the horse and overtook Anna on the level stretch in front of the lodge.

Trubee reined in and stopped the wagon. "Where *you* going?" he said.

"Away."

"That's what I was thinking—but where?"

"I don't know. Any place, so long's it isn't that farm."

"Climb up, and I'll give you a lift, then."

"You mean it?" Anna said.

"Sure I mean it. You don't want to be tramping around these woods all night, do you?"

"How do I know you didn't come after me?"

"You'll have to take your chances about that. Come on, miss, climb up. I'm on my way for a doctor, and I got no more time to kill."

The girl got up alongside of him, and Trubee let the horse have another belt with the whip. In a few seconds, they were rolling downhill so fast that Trubee had to stand on the brake to save the horse from getting run over by the wagon.

"Hold on tight," he said. "There's many a 'Thank you, Marm' between here and Bennett's, and we're going to take every one of them on the run."

The wagon banged down Harrington, tumbling like a loose barrel over the rocks that were halfburied in the road, slewing around the bends on its pigeontoed wheels, gnashing its tires on the free gravel, and fanning into wings the puddles that'd collected in the hollows. Twice they came within an ace of taking a spill, and both times they got away with it by luck, once when they ran into an outcropping root that righted the wagon just as it was going over into the bushes, and the other time when they actually did go over and were stopped by the trunk of a tree.

When they were half a mile above Bennett's, Trubee took his foot off the brake, which had been raining sparks off the tires ever since they left the lodge, and held the horse in to a trot for the long easy grade down to the farmhouse.

"When we get to Bennett's," he said, "I'm going inside and use their phone. You can push off for Warrensburg, and nobody'll see you if you don't want them to." He was quiet for a minute or two, and then he said, "Where you going to go after you hit the village?"

"I don't know," Anna said. "I wasn't thinking about it."

"Where you from?"

"A little place in Jersey, near Tuckerton."

"How far?"

"I couldn't say exactly. About four hundred miles, I think."

"Four hundred miles! Got any money?"

"I had two dollars, but I left that up to the house when I ran off."

"I guess I ought to make that up to you," Trubee said, sticking his hand into his pocket.

"What for? You don't owe me anything."

"Take it, anyway," he said, trying to put a few bills into the girl's hand. "Five bucks ain't going to break me, and it'll get you halfway home."

"Well, thanks very much, Mister Pell."

"Mister Pell! That's a rich one."

"Why?"

"Oh, I don't know. Haven't heard it for a long time. Here's Bennett's."

They drove into the dark grounds, and Trubee brought the wagon to a stop in the cave of trees that ran all the way from the road to the house.

Trubee jumped off, waved his hand to the girl, and said, "So long, miss. Take care of yourself." Then he started up the driveway.

"Please, Mister Pell."

Trubee came back. "Yes, miss," he said.

"About that man back on the farm. How long'll it be before he's up and around again?"

"Blame me if *I* know. Sixseven weeks, maybe—if he lives. Why?"

"Nothing," the girl said.

"Well, so long again. I'm losing time."

"So long, Mister Pell."

Trubee cut across the front yard to the stoop of the farmhouse and pounded on the door. Getting no answer, he stepped back and hollered up at the secondstory windows. After a few seconds the crack widened under one of them, and a head came through.

"Who's down there?"

"It's me—Trubee Pell. That you, Mister Bennett?"

"Yes. What's the trouble?"

"Got to use your phone right away. Somebody's hurt up to the farm."

"Not Walter, Trubee!"

"No, somebody else."

"Be right down."

Trubee put in a hurry call for Doc Slocum, who promised to pick him up at Bennett's inside of fifteen minutes. Trubee hung up, thanked Bennett, and was about to leave the house when the farmer stopped him.

"How you been, Trubee?" he said. "First time I seen you since you got married."

"I'll make a call on you one of these days," Trubee said. "Right now, I better be out on the road waiting for Slocum."

"Who got shot up?"

"Friend of mine. It was an accident. Say, Mister Bennett, could I ask you to look after the horse and wagon? They're out there in the driveway."

"Sure, Trubee. Pick them up any time you like."

"Thanks. Good night, Mister Bennett."

"Good night, Trubee. Regards to Walter."

Trubee started for the road, and on the way he passed the wagon. He was surprised to see Anna sitting just where he'd left her.

"Thought you was on your way," he said.

"I made up my mind I was going to go back."

"Come on off of there. Bennett'll be out in a minute."

He helped the girl off the wagon, and then the two of them walked out to the roadway.

"You're crazy," he said. "You don't have to go back up there. Act sensible and head for Jersey while the heading's good."

"I don't have anybody in Jersey."

"You don't have anybody here, either."

"So it don't make much difference."

"It makes a whole lot," he said, and then he pointed down the road. "Warrensburg's only a couple of miles that way. You can't miss it, and you'll make it in an hour. Take my advice."

As he finished speaking, the lowhanging mist down the road began to glare, and then two white plates of light showed through.

"You damned fool," he said, as the doctor's car approached them.

Slocum took both of them on, and they made the trip back to the farm in a little better than half an hour. When Trubee and Slocum got up to Flood's room, they found that he'd slipped the hairbrush and loosened the cord, and again he was bleeding like a pig. Slocum set to work right away, but Flood was so weak that he had to give him a stiff jolt in the arm to keep him going. The lower shot was only a flesh wound, and Slocum managed to close it up without much trouble; the one in the shoulder had chipped off some bone, and it was a long time before the doctor was able to fish out the splinters.

While Slocum was busy with the bandages, Trubee took Pilgrim outside and warned him not to do any talking when the questions started to fly. "Leave me do all the answering, and you might get away with it," he said.

"I'm terrible disappointed about not getting him in the works," Pilgrim said.

It was three o'clock in the morning before Slocum came down to the kitchen to clean himself up. After washing his hands and arms, he sat down at the table and opened a notebook. Trubee sent Pilgrim outside.

"In a case like this, Trubee," Slocum said, "I have to make a report to the State Police. Whenever a man's treated for a gunshot wound, the doctor has to make a report. Where's Walter?"

"Upstairs some place. I don't just know."

"Better call him, Trubee. I want to talk to him about the shooting."

"I wish Flood could talk. Then he'd tell you about the accident himself."

"I'd like to see your father."

"What for? I can answer anything you want to know."

"All right, suppose you tell me. I know you long enough to take your word, I guess."

"Flood got hurt when he started in cleaning the gun," Trubee said. "I was out in the yard when the first shot went off, and soon's I hear it I run for the house, but before I get further than a step or two I hear the second shot. When I get upstairs, there's Flood laying on the floor with the rifle alongside of him. He could still talk then, and he tells me about he'd been trying to clean the gun and how she went off in his hands and got him in the shoulder."

"He was shot twice, Trubee," Slocum said.

"I asked him about that before he passed out, and he says the second shot came about when he drops the gun on the floor. She's apt to do that if you wasn't being careful with her."

"What kind of a rifle was it?" Slocum said.

"A Savage."

"What action?"

"Lever."

"A leveraction?" Slocum said.

"Yes."

"And it went off the second time when it fell on the floor?"

"Yes."

"I see," Slocum said. "And then what happened?"

"Nothing that you don't know about. I tried to do something for Flood, but when I see it wasn't any good, I ride down to Bennett's and get you on the phone."

"Where was this other man when the accident happened?"

"You mean Pilgrim?"

"Yes, if that's his name. The little man."

"He was in the kitchen cleaning up. He was downstairs, anyway. I know he was downstairs because I could see him moving around through the windows. There wasn't anybody with Flood when the shots went off."

"How about the girl?"

"She was taking a walk."

"And Walter?"

"I don't know where he was, probably out in the barn."

"Who's the girl, Trubee?"

"A friend of mine."

"Where's she from?"

"Do you have to put that down, too?"

"No, I'm just asking."

"Why, Doc?"

"Oh, just so."

"I don't see where it makes any difference."

"It might make some."

"How?"

"Folks in town are talking. That doesn't help any."

"What's there to talk about? She only come up here yesterday."

"Well, it's all over town already. People have eyes, you know."

"Sure, and they have mouths, too."

Slocum closed his notebook and stood up. "How have things been going with you, Trubee? This is the first time I've seen you since you went away to France. I knew you were back, but you've been keeping mighty strange."

"Things are all right, I guess."

"The Piries moved away from Thurman, you know. They live over to Horicon now."

"I'm going up to see how Flood's getting along, Doc. How much we owe you?"

"No hurry. I'll be back late this afternoon to change the bandages. Want a lift down to Bennett's so that you can get your wagon?"

"No."

CHAPTER TEN

That afternoon, while Trubee was waiting outside of the house for the doctor to return, Pilgrim came through the kitchen door and headed for the road.

"Where you bound for?" Trubee said.

"No place."

"Slocum'll be along any time now. Let's walk down the road till we meet him."

"It's all right by me."

They covered half the distance to the lodge before either of them spoke again.

"I didn't fool him any," Trubee said.

"Fool who?"

"Slocum."

"About what?"

"The shooting. When I give him the story last night, I knew better than to think he was taking it all in."

"What did you tell him?"

"That Flood shot himself while he was cleaning the gun."

"Well, that *could* of happened, couldn't it?"

"Sure, if he only got shot once, or if the gun was an automatic, but when I tell Slocum that Flood plugs himself twice in a row with a leveraction gun, I'm as good as saying straight out that I'm a liar."

"Then what did you say it for?"

"What would you of said?"

"Anything, but I wouldn't of made him leery."

"I said the only thing I could, unless you think I should of come out and told him you did it."

"What'll Slocum do?"

"It's hard to say. He knows me since I was born, and if he takes it easy in his report to the police, you can be damned well sure that'll be the only reason for it. If he thinks I had something to do with the shooting, then he might call it an accident. But it's not Slocum's report worries me so much. It's Flood, and what he's going to do when he gets better. Seems to me like you ought to be on your way before he gets out of bed. I'm not kicking you out, mind you. It's just that there's no telling about Flood."

"I don't mind going if you say so, Trubee, but the girl goes along with me."

"I was meaning to talk to you about that."

"What's there to talk about? She's my girl, and she goes when I go."

"She's nobody's girl."

"No? Then maybe we should of let Flood finish up what he started last night. Maybe it was none of our business butting in."

"She don't have to be our girl for us to stop her from getting ripped apart."

"What's the use of you and me arguing, Trubee? I say Miss Wayne's my girl, and that's all there is to it."

"Like fun it is! You done the wrong thing bringing her up here in the first place."

"But she come up here because I sent away for her. Don't forget that."

"I'm not forgetting anything. I'm not forgetting you told her a pack of lies, either. She comes chasing up from Jersey thinking the lies was the truth, and just because it was you that made up the lies, that don't give you any hold over her that I can figure out. And just because she come up here looking for a James Pilgrim, that don't make her your girl. She wanted to light out the minute she laid eyes on the place, and she was right about it. She's nobody's fool. What should she stick around for? So's somebody can put the business to her whenever he feels like it? So's she can have the life scared out of her from morning to night? So's she can be chucked to Hell out when we get tired of her? If she wants to clear out, I say it's up to us to give her the carfare and see to it that she goes back to where she belongs. I'm telling it to you straight that there's nobody going to harm her while I'm around, and if you don't think I mean it, just get gay and see what happens to you."

Pilgrim laughed. "Giving me a warning, Trubee?"

"Yes."

"Maybe you're forgetting who shot Flood."

"If you want the credit for bagging him, you can have it, but just keep in mind what I said."

"Warnings don't scare me any, and I'll tell you why. I'm not such a brave guy, Trubee. Being this size, I can't afford to be. Being this size, I can't beat everybody up and slug them around to my way of thinking, like Flood did; but me being little, that never stopped no hard sonofabitch from messing me up whenever he felt like it. In my lousy life I got smeared hundreds of times, and there ain't much more for me to be ascared of. What's another sock in the jaw? What's another lug in the gut? What's another root in the tail? People been picking on me right from the time I found out how to walk, and they tramped all over me because there wasn't anything I could do to stop them. You'd puke if I told you about the whalings I've took in the past twenty years; you'd be sick to your stomach even if I only told you half. But don't make the same skull that Flood did: don't think that just because I'm a runt I'm yellow. You want to know the reason for this spiel? It's that I mean to take Miss Wayne away from here. I'm not such a lunk as to think I can drag her off by the hair, but she's got me so bad my tongue comes out and drags on the ground even when I'm only thinking about her. Nobody can stop me asking her to marry me, just like I said in the letters. Nobody can stop me doing that—not you, and not Flood, and not the two of you put together."

"Fair enough," Trubee said. "All I'm saying is that there's going to be no more rough stuff. And about the way you been treated all your life, I guess you haven't got any kick to make about me. I never lifted up a finger to you."

They waited on the porch of the lodge, and in a few minutes they heard the sound of Slocum's car from lower down the road. Slocum stopped for them and gave them a lift back to the farm.

Later in the day, after Slocum had gone, Anna came through the barn and stood on the runway looking out across the fields. She was wearing a faded yellow dress and lowheeled shoes, but no stockings. The wind blew the dress against her legs and bloomed it behind her like a parasol. The sun was in her eyes, and when she raised her hand to shade them, she saw Trubee sitting on the grassy mound that sloped away from the foundation of the building. He was watching her.

"Hello," she said.

"Hello, Miss Wayne."

"It's pretty nice out this afternoon."

"Always is around this time of year."

"How's that man feeling?"

"Martin? He's coming along all right. The Doc was worried about he might get lockjaw on account of the bullets was fired from so near, so he gave him a needleful for it. After a little while, he won't be any the worse off. He lost close onto a quart of blood, you know, but a couple of good juicy steaks into him and he'll get all that back."

Anna was looking away at the woods again by the time he'd finished talking about Flood.

"Ever been in the woods before?" he said.

"Not this kind. We don't have real woods where I come from."

"Maybe you'd like for me to show you around."

"I wouldn't mind," Anna said.

They crossed the fields, climbed over a rail fence, and entered the woods. Bearing to their left, they soon reached the deep groove cut by Stewart Brook, but instead of making their way to the road on the other side, they followed the watercourse up the gully toward Viele Pond. All they could hear was the sound of water pouring into pools.

Trubee pointed to a basin ahead of them and told Anna that if she went up to it very quietly she'd probably see some trout floating over the sand and gravel bottom. They went closer without alarming the three slowlywaving forms lying just off the run that made for the lip of the pool. A white shred drifted over the fall from the pool above, and all three of the trout shot themselves into the run for it. Trubee was suprised to see a bullhead waddle out from behind a rock and go after the food, too.

"Fat chance he has to get anything away from them trout," Trubee whispered as he watched the bullhead scull its pear-shaped body through the water. One of the trout darted toward it, and it bustled back to the rock. "They don't get any too good a living out of this brook, and when something tasty comes their way they don't give it up to any little catfish. I bet they keep him on a mighty strict diet down here; I bet he's feeling kind of sick being so far away from them nice mudholes up to the Pond. They don't get sucked over that dam so often, but when they do this is what happens to them. I used to fish them out and dump them back in the Pond .... See if you can watch the trout when I chuck this in."

He dropped a pebble into a still part of the pool. It made a small sound when it hit the water, as if it'd fallen on a china plate. Anna tried to keep her eyes on the trout, but they went out of sight so quickly that she didn't even know in which direction they'd gone.

"Well, where are they?" Trubee said, laughing.

"They're gone, that's all I know," the girl said. "They was here one second, and not the next."

"No use you even trying to watch them. As soon's I lifted up my hand, they was some place else. They don't wait on anything, and they sure can travel, by God. Look at the bullhead. He's coming out to have a sniff at the pebble."

They climbed up the rocks that lined the brook until they came to a small bridge made of logs. The bridge, Trubee said, was part of an old corduroy road that'd been laid down through the woods when his father was a boy. The road went up over a mountain to a forest of black walnut that'd long ago been lumbered. There were a few pieces of it still standing here and there, but not enough to make it worth Harry Reoux's while to cut it down and cart it to the railroad.

"Who's Harry Reoux?" Anna said.

"Chap from down in Warrensburg. He owns the lodge and all this property up here between my father's place and Bennett's. Must have tentwelve thousand acres of it."

"You were talking about a road. I don't see any road around here."

"It's buried by now, that's why. Here's a piece of it." Trubee kicked up a chunk of moss with his heel. Under it there was a layer of yellow punk. He picked up some of it, and it crumbled in his fingers like a piece of cake. "That's all that's left," he said.

Crossing the bridge, they went through a pinegrove to the dam and then followed the bank of the Pond to a small dock. They went out to the end of this and sat down. Leaning out over the water not far away from them was a clump of birches that looked like a giant bunch of celery. Trubee saw something move among the branches and told Anna where to look if she wanted to see a kingfisher. After a little while a grayblue stone fell out of one of the birches and smashed down between the lilypads. As it hit the Pond the stone grew wings, and smacking them hard on the water, it came up with a small chub and flew away into the woods.

"Hardly ever misses, that bird don't," Trubee said. "Seems to me like he's a sight better fisherman than them fellows with fancy poles and store rigging. When a kingfisher goes down, he brings something back with him pretty near all of the time."

"He puts me in mind of the fishhawks that fly around over the inlet where I used to live," Anna said. "Of course, the hawks don't move so fast, being better than five feet across, but when they make a strike you'd think a house was falling down on the water. They stay up about a hundred feet in the air, and they keep their head down, looking at the water and looking at the water, and then when they see something they want, they fold up their wings and stick out their hooks and fall—just fall. I saw some hit the water so hard that the whole bird went under and didn't come up for a couple of seconds. You'd think he drowned himself, he stayed down so long. When he came up, though, he had a fish that ran a sure two pounds, and it gave him a real battle, I can tell you. It was flopping around and moving this way and that, and for a while you couldn't tell which one was going to come off on top, the bird or the fish. The hawk was lifting himself up off the water a couple of feet, and then he was sinking right back again. Finally, he made off with the fish—a whiting, I think it was."

"They're pretty powerful, them ospreys."

"How did you know they were called ospreys?"

"I read about them in a book," Trubee said.

"Once I found a hawk's nest. It was 'way inland, maybe three miles, and up in the top of a big tree. I got as far as a branch right under the nest—it was a big nest, about as big as a clothesbasket—and then all of a sudden the hawks came out and made a terrible noise. They flew all around and screamed at me, and I got scared they were going to put those hooks of theirs in my face, so I climbed right down again, and in a pretty big hurry, I can tell you."

The only sound that came through the woods was the far-away falling of Stewart Brook. Frogs gulped from under the soft banks of the Pond, and around the hot planks of the little dock dragonflies scraped their isinglass wings.

Anna said, "Could we go for a swim here, do you think?"

Trubee had been watching a heron come down to the marsh across the water. Turning to the girl, he said, "Sure we could, but how we going to rig up some suits?"

"I was thinking maybe we didn't have to take off all we got on."

Trubee stood up. "I'll go back there in the trees. You holler when you get in the water, so I know it's all right for me to come out. But make sure you take a flat dive off the dock. It's only about three foot deep here, and you don't want to get tangled up with that mud on the bottom."

He went into the grove. It seemed very dark at first, like the inside of a barn after he'd been out in the fields for a long time. The old needles on the floor of the grove sank under his feet like fresh snow. When he reached a place that couldn't be seen from the dock, he took off all his clothes except the trunks of his underwear. After a minute or so, he heard Anna dive into the water, and then she called to him. When he got back to the dock, she was swimming about sixty or seventy feet out.

Trubee took a long shallow dive. As the water closed over his body, he felt as if it were exploding toward him, and for several seconds he lay stretched out in it just as he'd gone in. The cold spread out through him from his chest. His teeth turned to icecold pebbles, and there were icecold pebbles jammed into his ears. His eyeballs were agates, and the nails on his fingers and toes felt like frosted glass. He raised his arms out of the water and slapped them until the tightness went away. Turning over, he slid through the lilystems and came up near the girl, and then both of them swam out to the middle of the Pond, where there were no lilypads in the deep dark water.

When they were tired of swimming and diving, they lay on the water and paddled with their hands to keep themselves on the surface. Anna was wearing only a petticoat, and she had it tied so high up over her shoulders that the bottom of it didn't reach her knees. When she floated, with her stomach a little below the top of the water, the petticoat was plastered against her, and Trubee could see the color of her hair and the shape and color of her breasts through the thin white cotton. She looked as if she had no clothes on at all.

The heron was up in the air again, sailing slowly around the Pond in wide circles. It didn't come down while Trubee and Anna were in the water, but sometimes it coasted over them to see what they were. When Trubee beat the water with his hands and feet, the bird flapped its heavy wings and plodded away again. While watching it, Trubee saw a buzzard cruising far up in the sky. It rode the windcurrents and floated easily and very slowly down a broad spiral staircase in the air.

They stayed in the water until a herd of clouds rode up the comb of Black Spruce Mountain, a ridge running south from Stewart Brook, and hid the sun behind a booming bank of gray. After that, the air felt as cold as the Pond. Trubee was the first to climb out, and he went back to where he'd left his clothes. He took off the trunks and slapped himself dry, and then, after dressing, he waited for Anna to call him. When she did, he found her tying up her hair with one of the straps of her petticoat.

"I haven't felt this good in a long time," she said.

"Me, neither."

"The Pond's fine. It's a whole lot different to swimming in the ocean. It don't hold you up as good as salt water, and you have to swim a whole lot harder to get anyplace, but you feel better when you come out of it."

They went back to the farm by way of the road.

CHAPTER ELEVEN

Two days after the shooting Flood was running a fever of a hundred and two, but Slocum said that the reason for that was the injection he'd given Flood to prevent lockjaw; he told Trubee that outside of Flood's being uncomfortable for a week or so, there'd be very little to worry about.

The next morning Flood woke up roaring at the top of his lungs, and Trubee came down from the attic to find out what the trouble was. Flood had stripped the blankets off the bed and flung them on the floor, and all over the man's naked body there were little twisted burrows that stood up at least a quarter of an inch from the skin. The welts were raw and looked like worms that'd bored their way into Flood's flesh, and wherever Flood had torn at them with his nails they oozed a serum that quickly hardened into a crust like sap. Trubee had never seen anything like this before. He stood at the foot of the bed, looking down at the sick man.

"Do something for me, you dirty sonofabitch!" Flood shouted. "*Do* something! Don't stand there with your mouth open! Do something! Jesus, these things is killing me."

Trubee went downstairs and found Anna and Pilgrim in the kitchen.

"Sounds like Flood's cashing in, Trubee," Pilgrim said.

"And here we are stuck without a horse and wagon," Trubee said.

"Here *you* are, you mean. That guy's no worry of mine."

"I'll have to drive the liquor truck down to Bennett's and use their telephone again. I can't leave Flood hollering like that. If I could only think of something to stop that itch he's got."

"Is that what's the matter?" Anna said.

"Yes. This is a new trouble he's got now. It's with his skin, and he's digging it up with his nails like he aims to do some planting down there."

"Is there any baking soda around?" Anna said.

"Sure. There's a box of it in the cupboard. Why?"

"Get it for me, and I'll fix something up."

Anna dumped all the soda into a bowl, added some cold water from the well, and made a thick paste that looked like plaster.

"See if this does any good," she said.

Trubee took the bowl upstairs and smeared the sodapaste all over Flood's body. Then he sat around for a while, and he was surprised when Flood began to quiet down.

"Feel any better, Martin?"

"A little. What's that crap?"

"Baking soda and water. Miss Wayne mixed it up."

"Who?"

"Miss Wayne. I was just about to go for Slocum, but I guess we can wait now."

Later in the morning, when Slocum had come, Trubee told him what'd happened.

"Who made the salve, Trubee?" Slocum said.

"The girl."

"She still here?"

"Yes."

"I suppose you were pretty excited about Flood."

"Well, he had me worried there for a little while."

"Think he was dying?"

"Didn't think about anything. All I know's he sounded pretty bad."

"He sounded a lot worse than he was. He has the hives."

"The hives! Is that all?"

"That, and a couple of 30.30 bulletholes. You take the two together, and you have a man that isn't exactly ready to do a day's work."

"How'd he ever get the hives?"

"They sometimes come after an antitetanus injection. They'll annoy him for a while, but they won't kill him. It'll take more than an itch to bury that horse. Where's he from, Trubee?"

"Said he was born in Nebraska."

"Where do you know him from?"

"The army."

"What's he doing here?"

"I took him along with me. Got any more questions?"

It took more than a week for Flood's fever to get down under a hundred and stay there without the help of pills, and for many days after that he was weak and very quiet, and he just lay in bed looking up at the ceiling and paying very little attention to Trubee when he came into the room to give him his food or help him with the bedpan. Outside of Slocum, no one but Trubee went in to see how Flood was getting along. Neither Anna, Pilgrim, nor old man Pell would pass the bedroom door while it was open, but Pilgrim was the only one of the three who wouldn't even mention Flood's name.

One morning about three weeks after the shooting Trubee went upstairs with Flood's breakfast. Flood ate some of the food, and then he said that he wanted to talk to Pilgrim. Trubee was surprised, but he went over to the window and called Pilgrim in out of the yard.

The little man met him at the head of the stairs and asked him what he wanted.

"Flood's asking to see you," Trubee said.

Without saying a word, Pilgrim started down the stairs again.

"Wait a minute, Pilgrim. You're not doing the right thing. If I was you, I'd go in and see him."

"What for, Trubee? What in Hell for?"

"To see what he's got to say."

"His talk can't change nothing."

"How do you know, if you won't listen? Go on in. Go on in, like a good guy."

"If it'll make you feel any better, all right, then, Trubee."

Pilgrim went into the room alone and stood at the foot of the bed looking down at Flood.

"What do you want?" he said.

"I heard you and Trubee talking down the hall just now," Flood said.

"What about it?"

"I can't say I blame you for not wanting to come in here."

"I don't get you."

"I mean you did the right thing the other night, Jim. I'd of done the same if I'd been in your boat."

"I still don't get you."

"I mean I had it coming to me. Looking back, I can see where I was just spoiling for what I got. I'm apologizing to you, Jim. I'm saying straight out that I brung it all on my own self. I don't hold you to blame, and I don't want you to go around thinking I'm sore at you. You didn't do nothing nobody else wouldn't of done if they had to. I'm sorry I ever lifted up my hands to you, and I promise I won't never do it again. Even if I was in the right, I shouldn't of picked on a smaller man. I'm asking you to shake on it."

He held up his hand, but Pilgrim didn't take it.

"The way I look at it, Flood, you're no friend of mine, and you don't mean me no good at all. And me, I'm not making any secret out of trying to blow your guts out. That being the case, you can dope out for yourself just how much love I got for you."

"You're not saying anything I wouldn't say with things the other way 'round, Jim. You didn't get treated any too white by me, and I'm owning up to it."

"What good does that do me—you owning up to kicking me all over the lot like a dog? None that I can see. You could own up till you was blue in the face, but that wouldn't make me forget about them kicks you give me, or them clouts on the jaw. You didn't hit me with talk, and talk can't patch up what you done with them hands and heels of yours. I'm not crazy about you for trying to steal my girl away, and stepping all over my clock with them hobnails you got in your shoes. Come right down to brass tacks, you been a bastard all your life, so why should I kid myself you're getting soft now?"

"I been sick, Jim, and funny things come over a sick man."

"What do *you* know about being sick? Why, you wasn't sick a day in your life till three weeks ago. *I'm* the one can tell you what it means to be laying out on your back."

Flood turned his head away. "I'm sorry you're taking it so hard, Jim. I figured if I was to call you in here and try to make it up to you, you'd go a little easier. When a man's laid out, I guess the only thing he can do is talk, but it looks like you want more than that."

Pilgrim fidgeted for a couple of seconds, and then he said, "I never wanted no more than was coming to me, Flood, but I'm not shaking with nobody that there's something we got to settle up first."

Flood faced the little man again. "I'm willing to settle anything you say."

"This is a thing that we got to settle once and for all. It's all right you apologizing and saying you feel bad about you knocked me down and stood all over me face. Words can't sew up the gashes you put in my puss, and it can't take off the nailmarks, neither—but I didn't start in to talk about that. I don't care so much about getting beat up because, like I told Trubee the other day, that's what I'm used to. People always took a poke at me, and

I guess they always will, so I can get over you shoving me around like you did. There's something else I got on my mind, Flood, and that's Anna Wayne. I'm not so much on making speeches or handing out orders, but I mean it like I never meant anything in this bastard of a world when I tell you that she's my girl. I got the idea of sending away for her, I wrote all the letters, and I made up with her about coming here. Nobody else had nothing to do with that. She come looking for a James Pilgrim, and a little matter like me saying I was bigger or taller or stronger than I am, that don't change it none that when she come from Jersey she didn't know any Martin Flood from a hole in the ground. Or you happening to be here, that don't change it, neither. Trubee, he didn't butt in and try to steal her, and you can't be doing it just because she's a God damned swell piece and you got it all figured out you can bowl me over if I get in your way. She's *my* girl, I say, and if you don't think I mean it, just remember what I tried to do the other night. That's my little say, Flood. If you give me your word, as God's your judge, that Miss Wayne's my girl, I'll call everything quits and shake with you."

Flood raised his hand again. "Sure I'll shake on that, Jim. That was one of the things I was meaning to apologize about, only I didn't know just how to put it. I was wrong about Miss Wayne, same's I was wrong about all the rest."

Pilgrim ran around to the side of the bed and took Flood's hand in both of his own. He sat down alongside of Flood, and the two of them looked at each other and began to laugh. Then Pilgrim lit a couple of cigarettes and passed one over to Flood.

"Listen, Martin, what do you think of this for an idea—why don't *you* write away to Mrs. Wanda Kranz?"

From then on, Pilgrim took Trubee's place as far as waiting on Flood was concerned. He didn't ask for the job; he just took it over as a matter of course. He said that he'd put the man where he was, and that since Flood had turned out to be regular after all, it was no more than right that he should do all he could to help him out of it. From that time on, then, it was Pilgrim who helped Slocum with the dressings and bandages, and it was Pilgrim who changed the dirty bedding, and it was Pilgrim who gave Flood the bedpan and took it away and cleaned it out. As a matter of fact, it was Pilgrim who did everything for the sick man. He fed him, washed him, shaved him, combed his hair, brought him cigarettes and candy from Warrensburg, talked to him, and read to him. When there was nothing special to be done, he hung around the bedroom on the chance that Flood might take it into his head that he wanted something in a hurry; and when Flood was asleep, Pilgrim went out into the fields and picked berries for him, and once he went up Stewart Brook with Trubee and caught a mess of trout to break up the diet of chicken and venison that Flood had been living on. The trout were small, none of them going to over eight inches, and Pilgrim saved every one of them for Flood; there were eighteen in the catch, and Flood said that he didn't want them all, but Pilgrim said that if he couldn't eat them for supper, he'd get them for breakfast, and that if there were any left after that, he'd get them again for dinner—but no matter what he did with them, nobody else was going to get even a bone.

When Pilgrim wasn't doing anything special for Flood, he sat up in the bedroom with him for hours on end, talking, cracking jokes, reading stories out of the magazines that he'd taken from the lodge at Viele Pond. He told Flood all about himself, where he was born, who his parents were, the lousy time he'd had when he was young, how he'd happened to become a jockey, the different places he'd been to all over the United States, Canada, Cuba, and Mexico; he told Flood what he expected to do in the future.

He took it for granted that when he left the farm with Anna, they'd get married as soon as they ran across a parson. He wasn't very clear about what he was going to do after that, but he did say that he was playing around with the idea of hitting Saratoga for the August racing season, or going on to New York if he missed the Saratoga meet. He might be able to land a job with some trainer, he said, or at least find work as an exercise boy until something better came along; he still knew all he'd ever learned about racehorses, and that'd easily be enough to open the way to some kind of living around the tracks. There was one thing about horseracing, he said, and that was that there was always a place in it for an old hand. He'd always been pretty fair when it came to conditioning horses, and there was nothing very much in the way of his catching on with one of the big stables. If he got into hot water on account of having been ruled off as a jockey, he had his honorable discharge from the army to help him wipe that little black mark off the books.

He couldn't understand why Flood had refused to have anything to do with the True Blue Club. He'd tried to argue with the man, telling him that the chances were that he'd have good luck, too, and that maybe he'd draw himself a number as neat as Anna, but Flood had said no, and that was all there was to it. It was Flood's funeral after all, and if he wanted to have a go at it all by himself, there weren't going to be any complaints from a guy who'd been lucky enough to find something better for the winter than an extra blanket. He had his woman, so why should he worry? If Flood got too hard up, he'd know what to do about it. The only thing, though, was that dames like Anna didn't grow on trees.

Flood said very little, and when he did talk it was seldom about himself. He hadn't been much of a talker at any time, and now that he was sick the others didn't expect him to go shooting his face off. They did what they could to make him comfortable, and from the way he acted he seemed to appreciate their putting themselves out for him.

During all this time, Pilgrim was making weekly trips to Warrensburg with packages of whisky. He'd found a few more customers, and on each trip now he was taking down about two cases of the Johnnie Walker. The money rolled in, and Trubee took care of it for the three of them, holding out only enough to cover the running of the house. He counted the money one day about four weeks after the shooting, and he found that he had almost two hundred dollars in the tin can that he was hiding the savings in.

The same afternoon, Pilgrim put an extra large order into the wagon and covered it over with a piece of canvas. Then, waving to Flood, whose bed had been moved close to the window, he started up the road toward the Pond. When he'd covered a good part of the distance, he caught up to Anna, who was walking in the direction of the lodge. He stopped when he reached her and asked whether she felt like taking a ride to Warrensburg with him. She said that she did.

It took more than an hour to make the Schroon River bridge, and during that time neither the girl nor Pilgrim had a word to say. For Pilgrim's part, there was nothing to talk about. When he got Flood on his feet again, he'd give Anna the word, and they'd be on their way; in the meantime, all he had to do was dream about their married life. That's all he had to do—just dream about it. When the time came, he'd take Anna and his share of the whisky money, and then they'd chuck their stuff into a bag and kiss the farm goodbye.

Jersey couldn't hold a candle to the Adirondacks. It was pretty—sure it was pretty—what with the inlet, and the beach, and the ocean, and the nice little trees, and the nice little farms, and the nice little hills. But everything down there was nice and little—that was just the trouble with it. If you wanted to see a mountain, you had to take one of those bumps they had in the fields and think it up a couple of thousand feet in the air, and if you felt like being in a forest, all you could do was go and sit in some apple orchard and do the rest of it inside of your head. When they talked about a mountain up here in this country, they meant something that it'd take you all day to climb up to the top of, not just some runty little knob that gave you a look at the roof of the barn. When they talked about a forest, they didn't mean any wornout patch of scrub; they meant miles and miles of trees growing so thick together that you had to work your way through them just as much with your arms as with your legs: they didn't mean any nice little park, with lawns and flowerbeds and gravel walks; they meant a place that was dark even in the daytime, where you heard sounds that scared you because you couldn't ever tell what'd made them, where things shot out from the brush and ran across your way so fast that they were gone before you could tell their color, where you always felt like you had to go on and on without touching anything or sitting down, because you thought every twisted root might turn out to be a snake.

By Jesus, if there was a luckier guy in the whole wide world, he'd sure like to meet up with him. But what was the use of thinking about it, even? There was no such guy—there couldn't be. First of all, look at the form. It was enough to make a dead man sit up and eat his way out of the ground, and it wouldn't make any neverminds if he'd been laying there for a year, because when a dame like that one came along he'd just have to get up and do something about it. Look at the form. Look at that pair of peaches on her chest—no, plums, plums, because peaches were rough and made you go on edge when you sank your teeth into them—plums, that's what they were. Now, first of all, take a squint at that form.

After the wagon had passed the lodge, it went through an alley of beeches. The trees were close to the roadside in a swamp of peacolored ferns that sprayed up like great shuttlecocks.

It was much prettier in the mountains. Look at them 'way off there stacked against the sky like a mussedup deck of cards, every one a different color. Every one a different color! Now, wasn't that funny? Just like the sand on the beach, only here you were talking about mountains, not little grains of broken glass and rock. Every one a different color! Just look at them, the way they faded off from green to gray, through every shade of blue and lavender that you'd ever seen!

Brown, she was. Any place you looked, you saw brown— brown hair, brown eyes, brown skin, a bunch of brown freckles on her cheeks and nose. When he got a chance, he'd kiss every one of them freckles. When he got a chance...! When the Hell would he *ever* get a chance? How'd she like it when he shoved that pimply puss of his right under her smeller? By Jesus, maybe that was why she'd made believe she didn't like him the day he met her at the Lake George station. He should of knowed what was going to happen. As soon as she started in to write to him, he should of took a peep at himself in the mirror. If he'd of done that, then he could of got right to work cleaning up his stinky-looking skin. Why, she was probably thinking that he looked like a lousy squash, what with all them lumpy pimples busting out of his puss. Well, it wasn't too late yet, only he should of got busy on it a long time ago, and then he wouldn't of had all this trouble. When they got down to Warrensburg, he'd fix himself up with a box of something from the drugstore, and if the pills turned out to be no damned good, then he could plank up a couple of bucks and go see a doctor. But, Jesus, he could kick himself. Why the Hell didn't he think of that map of his before?

The wagon crossed the river, and Pilgrim headed north toward the village.

"You know, miss," he said. "I been meaning to tell you something for a long time."

"What?"

"Well, them lies I told you in the letters."

Anna said nothing. She was looking up the road.

"About them lies I told you," Pilgrim said.

Anna looked at him for a second. "What lies?"

"You know, the lies I said about myself?"

"You told me lies about yourself? When?"

"It's mighty nice of you to make out you don't remember, miss. I'm talking about where I said all them things about owning the farm and being six foot tall and having money in the bank—you know."

They passed a white church, a small frame building set in a bank of lavender hydrangeas. Anna followed the flowers until they were out of sight. Pilgrim looked at the church.

"It's sure nice of you to take it like this," he said. "Another girl, now, she wouldn't be so easy on me."

"Easy on you for what?"

"Oh, bringing you up here."

Anna stared at him. "You think a girl would go hard on you for that!"

Pilgrim wagged his shoulders and pouted. He wanted to smile, but he remembered his teeth. "She might," he said.

"Well, *I* wouldn't," Anna said.

This time Pilgrim couldn't hold back the smile. "You mean you're not sore at me, not even a little bit?"

"Sore! I should say not."

"You're glad I brung you up here?"

"Yes."

"Jesus!" Pilgrim said, slapping the horse into a trot.

CHAPTER TWELVE

Not until the fifth week was Flood allowed to get up and try to stand on his feet. He'd lost about fifteen pounds while lying in bed, and he was very unsteady the first time he took a few steps across the room, leaning on Pilgrim's shoulder for support. Moving Flood's bed down to the parlor was Pilgrim's idea; he said that Flood would be able to go outside and stretch his legs whenever he felt like it, without having to climb up a whole flight of stairs when he came back all fagged out.

The first week that Flood was downstairs, Pilgrim wouldn't let him go further than the barn or the road; he said that Flood had no business to strain himself by doing too much right off the bat, and that if he had any sense at all he'd know that the easier he took it at the start the better off he'd be in the long run. During the second week, Flood and Pilgrim went off on short walks through the woods or up the road toward the lodge. Flood was now beginning to have something left after the exercise, but Pilgrim kept at him to save his strength and tackle nothing that might set him back. Flood was annoyed with himself for not being able to do as he pleased, but he took Pilgrim's advice because he knew that whatever the little man said came straight from Slocum.

Pilgrim had lugged a couple of rockers out behind the barn, and one morning he and Flood were sitting there and dozing in the sun when old man Pell came out of the woodshed and passed behind them on his way to the house. They heard his footsteps, but neither of them bothered to turn around. Pell came back.

"How you feeling today, Flood?" he said.

Flood and Pilgrim stared at each other. It was the first time that Pell had spoken to Flood since the night of Anna's arrival at the farm, and it was also the first time that he'd asked anyone about Flood's health.

"How you feeling today?" he repeated.

"Coming along, I guess," Flood said. "It's mighty nice of you to ask."

"Feeling good and strong again?"

"Maybe not so strong as usually, but doing pretty good, considering."

"Doing pretty good, you say?"

"Well, a man don't stay sick so long with the kind of care I been getting."

"Glad to hear it," Pell said. "How about getting up off of your backside and doing some work?"

"Work?" Flood said.

"Yes, work. You know what that is, don't you?"

Flood turned away and looked across the pasture. "Sure I know, old timer, but why pick on me now?"

"Because you been grafting long enough, that's why. You been living off of me for a couple of months, and I want to tell you I'm sick and tired of it. You haven't done a lick of work since you come up here, but all the time I been slaving away harder than ever. What right have you got to be sitting in the sun like you owned this whole shootingmatch? I want you to do your share, or clear out."

"You're not being very sociable, farmer," Flood said.

"I never been sociable to you, and you know it. I never wanted you here in the first place, and the sooner you go back to where you come from the better it'll suit me. You don't belong here, and the only thing you're good for is boozing and starting trouble. I don't know what hold you got over Trubee, but you've took a mighty promising boy and sent him to the dogs."

"Don't get so overheated. You're barking up the wrong tree. I got no hold over Trubee, and I never did have. If you don't believe me, you ask Jim, here."

"Martin's telling the truth," Pilgrim said. "Trubee don't owe him nothing that I know about."

"He does whatever you want him to," Pell said to Flood, "and that's enough of a hold for me."

"Well, you can't blame me if he's yellow."

"He never was yellow till he met you, and I don't believe he's yellow now, but no matter what *he* is, you're a far cry from scaring me. This farm's still my property, and either you behave yourself or you get out."

Pilgrim watched Flood, who looked up at Pell for several seconds before speaking again.

"I'm sorry I said that about Trubee. He's been mighty good to me, and I wouldn't want him to think I don't regard him for it. When you come right down to bedrock, Pell, we *didn't* do the right thing about helping you out. We should of pitched in and did our share, and then nothing would of happened. I'm not so strong on my feet yet, but you just give me another week or so and I'll be starting something."

Pell walked away without saying anything more.

"Did you mean that about pitching in and starting something, Martin?" Pilgrim said.

"Sure I did, Jim. I don't say nothing I don't mean."

While Flood was sick, Trubee and Anna had gone up to Viele Pond many times. They'd built a raft out of fallen timber and floated it out to the middle of the Pond, where it was anchored with rocks tied to lengths of clothesline. Whenever they were tired of swimming, they hauled themselves up on the raft and lay in the sun. Nobody ever came up from Warrensburg while they were at the Pond, and they had the place all to themselves.

One day they were dropped off at the lodge by Pilgrim, who was on his way to the village to buy some provisions and deliver another few cases of whisky. Trubee and Anna had their lunch on the dock and then swam out to the raft. After sitting around for a while, Trubee got up and was about to try a dive when he heard his name roll out across the water. He saw Flood beckoning to him from the dock. He turned to Anna to say that he'd be back in a few minutes, but she told him that she'd go along.

When they reached the shore, they went up to the pinegrove and sat down on a sunny patch of needles near the dam. Nobody said anything for a time. A chipmunk came out from behind a rock and sat sideways on it; it prayed with its forefeet, like a kangaroo. Trubee bounced a pinecone off the rock, and the little animal tumbled all over itself trying to get away.

"Miss Wayne," Flood said, "I want to apologize to you, like I did when I made up with Pilgrim. You got a lot of apologies coming to you, but mostly from me. I'm sorry for the way I acted when you come up here to the farm, and if you say you don't hold it against me none, I'll be feeling a sight better than I do."

"I don't bear grudges, Mister Flood. So long as you say you're sorry, then I'm not mad any more. I guess I was more scared than mad, anyhow. Nobody ever treated me like you did, and it got me scared. But I been talking to you right along now, so you know I'm not scared any more."

"That's mighty white of you, Miss Wayne," Flood said. "You can bet your bottom dollar you won't have no more trouble out of me."

"And if you ask me," Trubee said, "it's mighty white of *you*, Martin, to be apologizing all along the line this way. Another man, even if he was in the wrong, he wouldn't take shooting off of anybody. I feel like shaking hands with you myself."

"Then what's stopping you?" Flood said, holding out his hand.

"It feels like you got pretty near all your power back again," Trubee said. "I can't put a dent in your fist any more than I could in a stone, so I guess you're as good as you was before all the trouble started. I can tell you I'm mighty glad about it, too."

"Thanks, Trubee."

"Now's as good a time as any to tell you about something that's been on my mind ever since that day when you called Pilgrim in the room and made up with him. How about you, me, and Pilgrim doing some real work around the farm? Pilgrim don't know an awful lot about it, but us two can show him. It's just about time we all started in doing something, anyhow. Why, with the three of us pitching in and giving my father a hand, we could make that farm the best one in the whole county. We'd run it all together, share and share alike. Miss Wayne, here, she could stay on as a kind of a hired girl, only she wouldn't get any very hard work to do. She's got no other place to go to, and we all made friends again, so why shouldn't she stick around and boss the kitchen? At least we'd know what a square meal was like again, because when you get right down to it there ain't anybody can fix food like a woman can. With somebody like her taking care of the eating, the four of us men, we sure could tear up plenty of ground. What do you say, Martin?"

"I say it's the best thing I heard in many a long day. I say it's the best idea you got in your whole life, Trubee. I'm with you all the way, and we can ask Jim about it when he comes home. How about you, Miss Wayne? Would you want to stay up here with us?"

"I guess I would," Anna said. "Trubee was right when he said that about me not having a place to go, and I was getting to like it up here, anyhow. If we all did some work, then Trubee's father could take it easy. He's not so young any more, and he won't be getting younger."

"Then it looks like it's settled," Trubee said. "By God, I feel better than I did in years. I feel like starting in to sing a song."

Flood and Anna laughed, and then Flood stood up and said that he was going back to the house to cork off for a couple of hours. All three of them shook hands on the bargain, and then Flood went away through the woods.

When Flood got back to the farm, he went into the parlor and locked the door behind him. He took off all his clothes in front of a mirror that hung between the two side windows of the room. After looking at the scars in his shoulder and groin, he put his heels together and stood up straight. Slowly, with his hands coming palmup from his sides, he took a long deep breath and held it for more than a minute, all the while examining himself in the glass. His body was narrow at the waist and hips, and broad across the shoulders and chest. There wasn't an ounce of fat on his gut, which he'd sucked so far in that his ribs stood out in a clear series, like the spread wingfeathers of a hawk. The muscles in his calves bulged as if they were flatirons that'd been shoved in underneath his skin, and his biceps were so round and hard that they looked like stuffing for his arms. Under these there were pits deep enough for him to have lost his fists in.

He did nothing but breathe deeply for several minutes, and then, slowly and carefully at first, but with increasing power as he made certain that he wasn't straining, he went through a number of exercises. The sweat came out of him and covered his body with a thin shine, but he didn't stop his bending and stretching for more than an hour. At the end of that time, he dried himself off and went over to a window for some more deep breathing. When that was finished, he put some clothes on, unlocked the door, and lay down on the bed. In a few minutes, he was asleep.

CHAPTER THIRTEEN

The next morning Trubee spoke to his father about the idea of running the farm on shares. The old man had nothing to say to him until he was finished, and then he shook his head.

"I'm dead set against it, Trubee," he said.

"Why, pop?"

"Because I can't see the point of taking on a couple of strangers when there's any one of a dozen that I could name down to Warrensburg that'd be only too happy to move in here and give you a run for your money. The people you work a farm with has got to amount to something. You can't expect to get the right kind of help out of any Tom, Dick, and Harry you happen to run across."

"So what you're kicking about is Flood and Pilgrim."

"Yes, and I'm not making any bones about it, neither. That lowlife Flood, I don't fancy him now, and I never will."

"You're making a big mistake about Flood. You don't know him like I do. He's a changed man since the shooting, and if you don't want to take my word for it, you can ask Pilgrim or Miss Wayne. He had the idea he could run the show up here without himself doing a stroke of work, but that's all over now, and I'm willing to vouch for it. He's gone and made apologies all around, even taking the blame for the shooting, saying he had it coming to him all along. If that ain't making amends, then I don't know what is. Why, the man don't even talk like he used to."

"You can say what you like, Trubee, but you'll never bring me around to admire him. Soon's I clapped my eyes on him I knowed he didn't belong to this neck of woods any more than an elephant, and you can't tell me that a couple of bulletholes into him is going to change that little fact. I know better, and I told him where he got off only the other day; I told him he ought to go back where he come from."

"You shouldn't of done that, pop. We made up the plan yesterday."

"You mean it's all settled?"

"Pretty near. I was banking on you giving us your leave."

"Well, you'll never get it, you can rest assured of that. I can't stop you doing what you feel like with your ma's forty, but there's going to be no sharing of *my* land—not while *I'm* alive. What do you think I been sweating out all this good blood for? Not for strangers, not on your tintype. If a man don't have none of his own flesh ready to take over some time, then he might as well admit he's been wasting his time. He hasn't got a damned thing to show for his work, and he's just been busting his back all for nothing. He's just been putting a lifetime of sweat and blood into the ground for the benefit of some stranger, a lifetime of sweat. That ain't my idea, Trubee, and I don't mind telling it to you. You'll never get my leave to take land that's been in the family for a hundred years and upwards and split it up with a couple of army bums."

"I was in the army, too," Trubee said.

"Yes, and you was in it without my leave."

"Did you ever stop to figure out why I run off that time and joined up with the army?"

"Didn't have to do any figuring. Esther told me what you said that time you called her down to Lake George. You waltzed off because somebody looked slanty at you. A fine reason for leaving a wife in the lurch—just because some hotheaded young squirts wouldn't talk to you!"

"Is that what you think, pop?"

"What else is there? You lit out because you didn't want any-body to say you was hiding behind a woman's skirts. You'd of been a sight braver to of stayed."

"If that was all there was to it, I *would* of stayed."

"The next thing you know," the old man said, "you'll be telling me you ran away on account of you had a terrible strict father."

"I don't see where suspenders is any better than apron strings."

"What do you mean by that?"

"Forget it," Trubee said. "We was talking about the plan. If it goes through, then I stay here; if it don't, I quit, and I quit for good. I'm not sore or anything, but it strikes me like you don't even know your own mind. You want me to work on the farm, but you wouldn't do the only thing you can to keep me here."

All of a sudden the old man threw up his hands and said, "Have it your way, Trubee. Have it your way." Then he walked away.

Early that afternoon Trubee started for Bennett's to arrange for the renting of a few pieces of farm machinery. He said that he was going on to Warrensburg after finishing with Bennett, and that he'd probably be back to the farm around suppertime.

Old man Pell watched the wagon until it was out of sight up the road toward the lodge. Then he looked for Anna, and finding her on the porch, he told her that he wanted to talk to her. She followed him out behind the woodshed, and when they got there he put his hand into his pocket and pulled out a roll of bills.

"If you know what's good for you, Miss Wayne, you'll take this money and clear out of this farm as fast as your legs can carry you."

"But why should I go, Mister Pell?"

"Because you're a nice girl, and I don't want to see anything happen to you."

"What could happen?"

"People like you oughtn't to be allowed to walk around free. You're bound to get in trouble no matter where you go or what you do, but up here's the worst place in the world that you could of picked out."

"I wish I knew what you're making all the fuss about, Mister Pell. I like it up here, and all the boys are good to me, so why shouldn't I stay?"

"Because you got a stick of dynamite in your hand, and you're playing with it like it was a roll of newspaper. Take my advice, and go 'way."

"I can't go 'way. First of all, I got no place to go, and second, the boys are counting on me to do my share."

Pell touched his hat. "Good luck to you, ma'am."

"Thanks," the girl said. "Well, I guess I'll be going back to the house now."

Pell watched her walk away. Then he looked down at the money, which he was still holding in his hand.

"Supposing you pass that over to me," Flood said.

The old man looked around quickly.

"Look again," Flood said.

Pell did so, and finally his eyes fixed on the door of the outhouse. He watched it swing open. Buckling his belt, Flood came out and walked over to him.

"You couldn't of picked a better place, farmer," he said. "I had a grandstand seat."

"A grandstand seat for what?" Pell said.

"Come on, now, farmer. Don't act so cute."

"I don't know what you're talking about. A grandstand seat for what?"

"The play you're making for the hired girl."

"You keep a civil tongue in your head, you loafer!"

"Don't try to sneak out of it, Pell. I seen you making a play for Miss Wayne."

"You're crazy."

"Crazy like a fox. Didn't I see you trying to give her money to go off with you?"

"You didn't see nothing of the kind."

"My, my. Wait'll Trubee hears about his old man is chasing around. Wait'll I tell Trubee his pop wanted to run off with the servant girl."

"I don't know what you're coming at, Flood, but you know full well what *I* was doing. I wanted to give Miss Wayne this money so's she could get out from under *you*."

"That's all I wanted to hear you say," Flood said, and then he bounced the boulder of his fist off the point of the old man's jaw, knocking him stiff into a stack of billets under the woodshed. Pell's head hit the sawed edge of one of the split pieces of timber, slashing open his scalp just above the ear. His body slipped to the floor of the shed, sat upright for a couple of seconds, and then rolled over into the thick mat of pale yellow chips.

Flood looked around, and seeing nobody, he picked Pell up, carried him over to the outhouse, and dumped him onto the seat. Then he went outside, closed the door, and headed for the front yard to look for Pilgrim. He found him sitting on the side steps of the porch.

"Come along, Jimmy," he said as he passed by. "I got something important I want to tell you about."

"Sure, Martin, sure," the little man said, and then he followed Flood through the meadow across the road from the house.

On the way, Flood talked about the new idea for running the farm and made believe that he was leading up to the important thing he had to say. When they reached a grove about a hundred yards from the house, Flood turned on the little man, grabbed him by the throat with his left hand, and let him have a heavy shot in the face with his right. Pilgrim flopped into the long grass, rolled over, and sat up with a look of complete surprise.

"Did you go bats, or something, Martin?"

"I been waiting two months for this, you sawedoff sonofabitch!" Flood said. "Get up, or I'll kick your ribs in."

Pilgrim started to stand up, saying, "Martin, I don't...," but the word *understand* backfired in his throat. While on his hands and knees, he was booted in the teeth.

Pilgrim screamed through the blood and broken bone that clogged his mouth. He tried to stand up once more, and this time Flood let him get all the way to his feet before dropping him again with a cannonshot to his belly. The little man lay flat on his back and looked up at Flood.

"Going to get up again, Martin, and when I do you better kill me." He choked on some blood and began to cry. "You better kill me, because if I live, you won't, you dirty lousy bastard!"

"I'm not going to kill you, Turd, but I'm going to put you where you put me—and without a rifle."

Pilgrim was on his feet again, still looking straight at Flood. "I never been ascared in my life," he said, "and it'll take more than a heel like you to make me beg." He made no attempt to protect himself with his hands and arms. He didn't try to run away. He knew that he was as helpless as a target, and he just stood there and waited.

"Come on, you bastard!" he said. "Don't be yellow."

Flood swung so hard that his feet left the ground. The punch mashed Pilgrim's lips back against his teeth and almost squeezed them insideout. His head hit the ground, making a sound like a piece of fruit squashing on a sidewalk.

Before he passed out, he managed to bubble through the chilisauce oozing from his mouth, "You dirty lousy bastard!"

Flood went over to the body and kicked it one in the side. He heard a rib crack like pencilwood. Then he bent down and picked up the body by the back of the neck. He held it away from him, and it slumped like an empty suit of clothes. With his free hand, Flood took Pilgrim's left arm and twisted it until it jumped in its socket. Then he gave the remains of the little man a final smash square in the face and dropped him into the grass. The body looked as if it'd been caught in a stampede. All that could be seen of the face was a bloody pulp, from which stared a couple of glass buttons as shallow and blind as those of a stuffed owl.

Flood wiped the blood off his hands and went back to the farmhouse. Not finding Anna, he went up to her room and listened at the door. He heard her humming a song. He opened the door and went inside. The girl was washing herself at the basin that stood on the commode. She was naked. When she heard the sound of the door, she swung around to see who was there. Her face was covered with soapbubbles that sidled down her cheeks. One large bubble, taking many smaller ones with it, wound itself along her jawbone until it joined a cluster at the tip of her chin. The sun went through the turning globe of water, lighting it like an electric bulb, and then it burst.

Flood walked over to the girl and felt her body with the palms of his hands, up and down her back and sides, over her breasts, along her legs. He took a towel from the rack behind her and wiped her face and the spots where the soap had dripped to her shoulders and chest. Anna was too frightened to cry. When Flood took his hands off her to undress himself, she backed into a corner and tried to cover her body with her hands and arms. Flood sat down on the bed. He patted the blankets and told the girl to come over and lie down. She stayed where she was, staring at him.

Flood patted the bed again, saying, "Come on over here and lay down, or do I have to drag you by your hair?"

He unbuttoned his shirt and pants and took them off. Then he took off his shoes and socks and stood up next to the bed with only his underwear on.

"You coming over?"

The girl stayed in the corner, pressing into it as if she meant to push herself out through the wall.

"Please, Mister Flood," she said. "Please."

Flood yanked his arms out of the underwear and then trampled it off him. He went over to the girl, picked her up out of the corner, and threw her down on the bed.

"Please *don't*," she said. "Please *don't*, Mister Flood."

Flood lay down alongside of her.

It was a solid hour before old man Pell opened his eyes, and after that it took him half as long again to get up enough strength to stand on his feet. He pushed open the door of the outhouse, and lowering his head before the brightness of the late afternoon sunlight, he saw on the floor of the shack a hardening smear that looked like the drippings of a red candle. He put his fingers to the back of his head, and they came away with part of the waxy scab that was forming on the wound.

Becoming used to the light, he raised his head and looked about him. In the yard, opposite the side of the house, he saw Flood sitting on the ground and leaning back against the trunk of a tree. The man's hands were laced behind his head, and he was looking up through the leaves at the little changing spaces made by the wind. Pell made his way across the back yard to the door of the kitchen, and Flood remained as he was, giving no sign that he'd heard the sound of the old man's stumbling. Pell went through the kitchen and started upstairs.

At the head of the steps, which he'd climbed in the slowmotion of a movingpicture comedy, he stopped to listen to Anna's buried crying. He knocked on her door, but the girl kept on crying and said nothing in answer to the knock. He looked into the room. He saw the girl's naked body on the plowedup bed. Her eyes were wide open, and she was biting the pillow. There was blood on the sheets.

The old man closed the door quietly and went downstairs to the closet in the parlor. Loading a shotgun, he left the house and walked over to within a few yards of Flood. Flood stood up. He looked at Pell, and then at the gun, and then he turned his back on both.

"Did you do that up there?" the old man said.

"Sure I did, farmer. I hope you didn't think she belonged to Mister Pilgrim."

Pell jerked the forward trigger and shot Flood in the back from a distance of ten feet. The pattern was close at that range, and it opened up a hole the size of a bung. The load of buckshot spun Flood all the way around, and he got the other barrelful square in the bellybutton. He fell with his front parting like a wet paper bag, and he was dead before his body hit the ground.

The old man stared down at Flood for a couple of seconds, and suddenly his stomach closed up like a fist, and he puked all over his clothes.

Then, no longer realizing what he was doing, he dropped the shotgun and ran into the house to get the 30.30. When he came out of the door with it, he fired three times without waiting to lift the rifle to his shoulder. One shot clipped Flood in the mouth and sliced the front teeth out of his lower jaw; the other two blew holes in Flood's skull, scattering his brains in the grass. Then the old man walked closer to the body, and emptying the magazine into what was left of the face, he took the rifle by the barrel and hammered away at Flood's head until he'd turned it into a sloppedover mess of blood and splintered bone that looked like stewed plums.

Finally the stock of the gun broke off, and then, his overalls sprayed like a butcher's apron, he went over to the porch and sat down in a rocker. Still holding the barrel of the rifle, he rocked himself.

CHAPTER FOURTEEN

Trubee finished his business with the Bennetts at about three in the afternoon, but it was almost five before they'd hear of his leaving; they turned the visit into a social call, and it was so late when he finally broke away that he decided to leave the trip to Warrensburg for some other time.

It was very hot and still, and there was little wind on the east slope of Harrington. The trees moved only in great sections, slowly, like animals breathing. Trubee saved the horse by getting off the wagon and walking all the upgrades, and before long his shirt and the back of his pants were soaked through with sweat. He stopped the horse at the place where the waterpipe stuck out of the bank at the roadside. He went over to the barrel and twisted his head to let the pipewater run into his mouth and over his face and throat. The water was so cold that it stiffened his lips and made them feel like a couple of strange fingers touching his face. Taking his mouth away from the pipe, he stood with his hands on the rim of the barrel, looking down into the water. The inside of the barrel was padded with a thick layer of dark green moss that waved a little with the movement of the water. Its darkness made the water look very deep, and it was a long long distance to the bright blue china bottom on which a cloud rippled like a poached egg.

When Trubee drove into the yard and brought the wagon to a stop, the first thing he saw was Flood's body. For several seconds he sat where he was, gaping down at the carcass, and then suddenly he jumped to the ground and dashed toward the house. He slowed up to a walk when he saw his father sitting in the rocker and staring off across the fields. Saying nothing to the old man, he went up to Anna's room.

He opened the door and took a long look at the girl. She wasn't crying now, and although she was still naked, she made no attempt to cover herself. She looked at the doorway as if there were nobody in it.

"Pack your bag, Anna," Trubee said, and then without waiting to see whether the girl had anything to say, he went downstairs again, took all the money out of the tincan bank, let himself out of the house through the kitchen, and began to look for Pilgrim.

Passing the woodshed, he spotted a red blotch in the chips of wood around the chopping block. From this, a wavering line of red drops led away along the sandy path to the outhouse. Not finding Pilgrim in the shack, but noticing the stain on the floorboards, he scouted for the little man in the fields. When he finally came across his damaged body flung out in the long grass of the meadow opposite the farmhouse, he went down on his knees alongside of it and began to cry.

Pilgrim wasn't dead, but he was still unconscious, and Trubee, not knowing how badly he was hurt inside, picked him up with all possible care and carried him back to the barn. Bedding down the body of the stolen autotruck with a thick layer of hay, he laid Pilgrim out flat on it, cranked up the cold motor, and then drove out to the house.

He called to Anna that he was waiting for her, and in a few minutes she came downstairs carrying her straw suitcase and dressed in the same faded blue serge suit that she'd worn when Pilgrim met her at the Lake George depot two months before. She had the same hat on, the one with the flopping flowers and fruit, and she wore it in the same way, straight across the top of her head.

Trubee helped her into the cab of the truck, and as he drove out through the gate, he saw her turn her head for another look at the farm. She turned back very quickly and said nothing.

Trubee took Harrington carefully, but once they were over the Schroon River bridge and straightened out on the state pike, he gave the truck all she'd stand. He slowed down to go through Lake George, and beyond it he again clamped his foot down on the gas pedal as far as it'd go. It was a tenmile run from the lower end of the lake to Glens Falls, and Trubee made it in fifteen minutes.

He drove straight to the Glens Falls hospital and left Pilgrim there. From the hospital, he went to the railroad station and found that the Albany local was leaving in half an hour. After buying Anna a through ticket to New York, he took her to a restaurant and made her eat a sandwich and drink a cup of coffee. While they were waiting for the train, he opened the girl's pocketbook and stuffed it full of bills. The last thing he said to her was that when she got to New York she should go and see a doctor.

Trubee took his time on the way back to Warrensburg. He looked at the hills, the trees, and the sky. He looked at the color of Lake George, the smoke of the "Sagamore" as she steamed between the islands up the lake, the clouds hanging low over the water. He read the names on the mailboxes that he passed, he saw the peeling paint on the houses, he watched a brook that followed the road downhill to the lake. He looked at men tramping in from the fields, at cattle standing bellydeep in little ponds of rainwater, at the powerline running up Harrington through an alley among the trees. He looked at haystacks, farm buildings, gardens, plowed fields, outhouses, birds on the railfences and telegraph wires. He spotted some crows in a cornfield, a brown and white dog sleeping under a wagon, a mare with her foal staying close to her flank as she waded through a patch of long grass. He saw two little girls playing with hoops in front of a barn.

Trubee stopped the truck in front of the Sheriff's Office in Warrensburg. Inside the office, Smead was talking to Slocum and to the game protector of the district, a man named Robbins.

"Hello, Trubee," Smead said. "We was just talking about you."

"Hello, Ed. I got something I want to say to you."

"Want us to clear out, Trubee?" Slocum said.

"No. I want you to stay, and you, too, Robbins."

Smead said, "What's on your mind, Trubee?"

"I want to say something, and I want it to be legal. Don't you have a man that writes down things for the court?"

"Bertrand's the man for that," Smead said.

"Get him over here, will you, Ed?"

While they were waiting for Bertrand, Trubee sat in a chair and stared at the floor. The druggist came down the street about ten minutes after Smead had called him. Smead gave him a pen and paper and told him to write down what Trubee said.

"I'm ready, Ed," Bertrand said.

"All right, Trubee," the sheriff said.

"There was a man come up to the farm with me a couple of months back," Trubee said. "He was somebody I met in the army. His name was Flood, Martin Flood, and he was a damned bad actor. He tried to run the show up there to the farm, and I didn't mind that so much, but when he started in using them big hands of his on everybody that crossed him up, it got so that a man just couldn't stand it any more. Today when I got back from a trip to Bennett's, I found out that he'd gone and smacked my father over the head and knocked him cold. I went out after Flood with a gun, and I killed him deader than a doornail, and then I busted the gun to pieces over his dome. He was a bad actor, and I'm glad I did him in. I come down here to give myself up."

When Trubee finished talking, he looked at Doc Slocum. Slocum opened his mouth to say something to Smead, but he changed his mind and kept quiet.

Viele Pond, 1935

Made in the USA
Las Vegas, NV
16 October 2022

57437192R00100